A SWEET VICTIM
OF BITTER DISAPPROVAL

Judson would like to have his mother meet this lovely girl from Virginia.

But what would happen if he were to bring home a girl he picked up on the street? His mother would look at her with utter disgust and remorselessly turn her out in haughty triumph.

No, he could not let that happen to delicate Ariel, with her cameo face and star eyes. He could not bear the thought of seeing that poor girl swiftly thrust into the blackness of a dark, strange world.

Bantam Books by Grace Livingston Hill
Ask your bookseller for the books you have missed

#1 WHERE TWO WAYS MET

#2 BRIGHT ARROWS

#3 A GIRL TO COME HOME TO

#5 KERRY

#6 ALL THROUGH THE NIGHT

#7 THE BEST MAN

#8 ARIEL CUSTER

#10 CRIMSON ROSES

#12 HEAD OF THE HOUSE

#13 IN TUNE WITH WEDDING BELLS

#14 STRANGER WITHIN THE GATES

#15 MARIGOLD

#16 RAINBOW COTTAGE

#18 BRENTWOOD

#19 DAPHNE DEANE

#20 THE SUBSTITUTE GUEST

#22 ROSE GALBRAITH

#23 TIME OF THE SINGING OF BIRDS

#24 BY WAY OF THE SILVERTHORNS

#25 SUNRISE

#26 THE SEVENTH HOUR

#27 APRIL GOLD

#28 WHITE ORCHIDS

#29 HOMING

#30 MATCHED PEARLS

#31 THE STRANGE PROPOSAL

#32 COMING THROUGH THE RYE

#33 HAPPINESS HILL

#34 THE PATCH OF BLUE

#35 PARTNERS

#36 PATRICIA

#37 SILVER WINGS

#38 SPICE BOX

#39 THE SEARCH

#40 THE TRYST

#41 BLUE RUIN

#42 A NEW NAME

#43 DAWN OF THE MORNING

#44 THE BELOVED STRANGER

#45 THE GOLD SHOE

#46 THROUGH THESE FIRES

GRACE LIVINGSTON HILL
ARIEL CUSTER

*This low-priced Bantam Book
has been completely reset in a type face
designed for easy reading, and was printed
from new plates. It contains the complete
text of the original hard-cover edition.*
NOT ONE WORD HAS BEEN OMITTED.

ARIEL CUSTER

*A Bantam Book / published by arrangement with
J. B. Lippincott Company*

PRINTING HISTORY
Lippincott edition published 1925
Bantam edition / June 1968

2nd printing ...... July 1968	4th printing .. September 1970
3rd printing .... July 1969	5th printing .. November 1976

ISBN 0-553-02875-8

Published simultaneously in the United States and Canada

*Bantam Books are published by Bantam Books, Inc. Its trade-
mark, consisting of the words "Bantam Books" and the por-
trayal of a bantam, is registered in the United States Patent
Office and in other countries. Marca Registrada. Bantam
Books, Inc., 666 Fifth Avenue, New York, New York 10019.*

PRINTED IN THE UNITED STATES OF AMERICA

ARIEL CUSTER

CHAPTER I

ARIEL CUSTER stood for a moment on the old white pillared porch of her childhood's home and watched the wagon drive out the gate and down the road toward town with the last pieces of her grandmother's dear old furniture. They were being taken to Ezra Brownleigh's to be stored for her until some time in the dim and distant future when she should be able to wrest from the great unfriendly world a home and a spot to put them. Ezra Brownleigh had bought them in for her at the auction sale the week before.

It was very early in the morning and the sun was still making long slant rays of brightness over the old lawn between the oak trees, and shrubs. A mocking-bird was singing wildly sweet in the maple by the library window as if there were no such thing as sorrow and desolation in the bright world, fairly splitting his throat with praise; and in the intervals of his trills Ariel could hear the creaking of one wagon wheel as it lumbered over the ruts on the old Virginia road. It seemed to be lumbering over her stricken young heart as she watched it out of sight down the familiar road.

Suddenly the tears blurred into her eyes and her white throat stirred hysterically. It seemed as if she could not bear it. All that was left of the dear old home, every memento of precious father and mother and frail little grandmother who had lingered longest with her on the earth, was packed into that rickety wagon and going down the road to storage. Ariel caught her breath and

turned quickly inside the door. Not even the mocking-
bird must see her weeping. She was a Custer and the
Custers kept their pride and bore smiling what came to
them. She must not be weak nor faint-hearted. Besides,
was not God in His heaven? Was He not watching over
her tenderly, even though for the time it seemed as if He
had withdrawn His tender care? The faith of her grandmother was in her strongly. Somewhere ahead there was
brightness, or if there was not, there was the brightness
of eternity when her way of this pilgrimage was over.
She had no thought of blaming God for the trials, or the
darkness, or the hardships of the way she had to go to
meet Him. That she was on her way Home was a settled
fact in her mind which no sophistry could disturb. She
might have to suffer through a century more or less, but
the loyalty of her heart belonged to God and she was
one of those in whom Faithfulness is written large; who
would willingly "let on they died of typhoid fever"
rather than let the world think she had been forsaken by
her God. God couldn't forsake. That was the keynote of
her life. Whatever came was under His overruling hand,
and could never overwhelm because His grace was
sufficient. Therefore she was safe wherever and however
she might find herself.

Ariel was one of those rare girls somehow left over
from what the world whimsically calls with a smile and
a sneer, "the *Victorian* Age" though it is to be doubted if
ever the Victorian Age saw many like her.

She still had her hair, all of it, wonderful hair, long
and heavy with a glint of copper and a ripple in it that
caught the sunlight and turned it into spun gold. It
crowned her lovely head in classic lines that no mod-
ernist can achieve, and perhaps would be incapable
even of admiring. She had eyes of the clear translucent
blue of an aquamarine, and the delicacy of her features,
and the fervent vivid look of her would make one wonder to see her in a crowd.

Now, as she turned back to the empty echoing house,
sorrow clothed her as in a hallowing garment, and her
face wore an ethereal look; that look perhaps that her

young mother had seen in her baby face, and called her "Ariel."

She stood for a moment in the wide hall, that ran from front to back of the house, with its glass doors into the garden at the back and a glimpse of fields and hills beyond; the hall where her mother's feet had trod; where her own childish laughter had rung out; where her little grandmother had loved to sit in the deep old rocker in her rusty black silk and her fine sheer ruffles and cap, doing delicate embroidery while Ariel studied on a cushion outside the door and the kitten curled in a black and white ball at her feet. How the memories flocked!

There through the wide arch was the old parlor where she had practised her music at the old square piano, with mother-of-pearl flowers set in its polished rosewood above the keyboard. Like ghosts the old furniture came trooping back and peopled the empty rooms. The Chippendale desk! The gate-leg table! The portrait of grandfather over the mantel! It was as if their various spirits had stolen away from their new owners and crept back to bid her farewell.

There on the other side was her father's library where she had spent hours poring over his big volumes; while he wrote at his desk, and now and again looked up and smiled, and said:

"Having a good time, little girl?"

Back of the library was the dining room with windows on the garden and the sunshine flooding it all the morning. There had been blue willow plates against the landscapes on the wall, and the great old mahogany sideboard reached the full length of the space between the windows. If only she might have kept the sideboard! It was so beautiful and old and rare. It seemed so a part of her life and her family. But Ezra Brownleigh had said it would bring more money than anything else she had, and she needed the money so much! But perhaps she would some day save money enough to buy it back—when she had a home. Oh—*when* she had a *home*—!

With the breath of a sob she dropped upon her knees,

and a long ray of sunlight stole through the mullioned window over the front door and laid gentle fingers of gold upon her hair like a halo, as with clasped hands and closed eyes she prayed earnestly,

"Oh, dear Father in Heaven, I feel so frightened, and so lonely! Please take hold of my hand and go with me—!"

Then she went with swift steps over to the window seat where lay her grandmother's Bible beside an old fashioned travelling bag and picking it up opened it and tried to read through blurring tears. She had taken the Bible from her grandmother's chest of drawers just before the man had come to take the things away. It was bulky to carry, but she felt she must have it with her. It would not seem so lonely in the great strange city to which she was going if she might have grandmother's Bible.

And it opened of itself to an old tried and true passage that had given comfort many times before in days of stress:

"Fear thou not; for I am with thee: be not dismayed; for I am thy God: I will strengthen thee; yea, I will help thee; yea, I will uphold thee with the right hand of my righteousness."

A look came over her face like unto the look of her illustrious warrior ancestor whose painted portrait had been wont to hang on the wall above the stair landing. It was as if she had just received marching orders from her captain. She lifted her firm little chin and a light was in her eyes like one who sees a vision.

She was going forth to fight. She did not expect an easy way. But her Lord was with her, even unto the end. With determination she set her face to the going.

Quickly she ran up the stairs to glance into every room and be sure nothing had been left behind. All was clean and empty as befitted the house that was being handed over from the Custer family to a new owner. Not a bit of dust anywhere. Only a scrap of faded lilac ribbon fallen from the drawer when she opened it to take out the Bible. She picked it up quickly as something precious and hid it in her pocket. It was one of the ribbons from grandmother's old needle book. She must not leave it there for strangers to fling away.

She came down stairs swiftly, gave one last sorrowful glance about the empty rooms and went out, closing and locking the door. Once more she paused with her hand still on the key, and looked abroad at the day which was beginning to glow with Springtime. The mocking-bird in the lilac bush was answering the mocking-bird in the maple now, and an ache grew in her throat as she realized that she was going from it all forever; her home, her lawn, her lilac bush and her mocking-bird, out into an unknown world. In all probability she might never hear a mocking-bird sing from that lilac bush again.

Then she shut her lips tight on the sob that sprang in her throat, turned the key in the lock, and with one last glance at the distant hills just taking on their spring verdure in soft pastel tints, she picked up the old fashioned satchel that stood ready at her feet and started down the path to the gate, every step carrying her away from her childhood, her dear old home, and all that she counted dear in the world, every step bringing the tears to her eyes, and the ache into her throat.

But being a Custer she did not yield to her mood. She dashed the tears from her eyes, swallowed hard on the lump in her throat, and lifting her chin with a kind of finality she went out the gate and down the road, walking straight as a young sapling, her little patrician head held high. The morning was early, the dew yet on the young grass by the roadside, but not even a bird should see her go drooping away from Virginia. She would go forth as one goeth to battle, a shining mark for an enemy, but a valiant one.

She hastened her steps as she passed the old Breckenridge place. She had said a sad farewell to old Miss Sally, the sole remaining representative of that family, who had been dear friends with her family. She did not want to go over it again. If Miss Sally should spy her out of the window she would be sure to stop her for another last word, and perhaps a hot buttered roll or some delicacy to take with her, and Ariel felt she could not bear it.

But Miss Sally did not see her and she slipped by safely and reached the straggling village street without encountering any old friends.

She must stop at the Real Estate office and leave the key for the new owners. Then she hoped to escape to the station without more ado. There had been invitations to breakfast in plenty, and also to stay overnight, but Ariel had declined them all on the ground that there were things to do at the house and she would not have time in the morning to stop for a formal breakfast. She had not let anyone know that her last night was to be spent alone in the old house. They had thought that Dinah the old faithful Negro servant was to be with her, or there would have been protests too strenuous to resist; but Dinah had had opportunity to ride to her new home with a farmer who was driving that way the afternoon before, and the girl had insisted upon her going. In fact she had been glad to be alone for those last hours. Somehow they seemed too sacred for even Dinah to intrude upon. And so she had spent the night alone in the old country seat, empty of all furniture save the few things she had saved for her own, which had gone down the road that very morning to be stored indefinitely at Ezra Brownleigh's house for her.

The past week had been one long good-bye, and Ariel dreaded another word of it. Her Custer pride was worn almost threadbare. She must not let them suspect how her heart was failing her about going out into a world of uncertainty alone. Someone would try to take her in, or do for her, if anyone suspected, and that must never be. She was a Custer and she was a Christian, and she must face the world alone with God.

The minister had written to a cousin of his in the North who was librarian in a big city library and she had promised to take Ariel in and teach her to be a librarian. The minister had felt that the many years spent in her father's library reading to him and browsing among his fine collection of literary gems had well fitted her for such a position, and she was looking forward with a sad anticipation to the joy of handling books once more. Her father's books had been sold three years before to provide the necessities of life for herself and her grandmother during her grandmother's last lingering illness. Even the money from the books was every cent gone now. Ariel longed for books, and she felt that a life spent among them would not be like a life exactly among utter strangers. There would be sure to be some old friends among the volumes.

Ezra Browleigh had not yet come down to his office. It was early. He doubtless had not expected her to come so soon. So she left the key with the office boy who was shooting marbles in the path outside the step. She was glad to escape the kindly parting from the gentle old man her father's friend who would gladly have taken her in and made her his own child if he had had the means to provide for her. As it was he had told her that if everything did not go right she was to come right home to Virginia and he would take care of her. Ariel never intended to burden him with any care of herself, even though things went very wrong indeed, but she thanked him and smiled sunnily into his faded eyes till he cheered up, marvelling at the Custer courage, rejoicing in the valiant spirit.

Arrived at the station Ariel had almost an hour to wait for her train. There was plenty of time to run over to Aunt Janey Whiting's and get breakfast, or even to go as far as Martha Ann Gibbon's little cottage where she knew there was always delicious corn pone and plenty of fresh milk for breakfast, and where she would be more than welcome. But Ariel did not feel like eating. There seemed to be a door locked in her throat that prevented her from swallowing. It seemed to her she never would be hungry again. So after she had bought her ticket and checked her small ancient trunk she crossed the tracks behind the station and walked away down a willow-bordered road to the old bridge where the trees hid her from the village, and she could be alone and think.

The old bridge crossed a little stream that wound

down from the distant mountain and was sparkling now in the sunlight as she stopped and laid her arms on the rail looking down into the water.

The trees on either bank were softly dappled with small green leaves, and bordered the bright curving water with feathery foliage, deepening here and there into the rich dark green of the cypress and pine. Beyond was the mountain, blue and mysterious in its morning mist, with a brilliant sky above in which floated little lazy fleecy clouds. The beauty of it was like a pain in her heart as she looked upon it for the last time perhaps for years. A sudden realization came over her of how dear it all was, the sky and the trees and the water, her dear Virginia mountains, and what it would be not to see them any more, and once more the Custer courage almost failed her, and she bowed her head on the old bridge and prayed:

"Dear Heavenly Father, don't let me break down. Help me to be brave. I know you're going with me."

But bye and bye the peace of it all sank into her heart and she was able to look upon the familiar scene and drink it into her memory for a future time of need.

The distant whistle of the south bound train warned her at last that her time of waiting was almost over, and she hurried down the road and was ready to cross the tracks as soon as the Southern train was gone.

But she was not let to leave her home town absolutely uncheered. Miss Sallie Gibbons was standing on the platform anxiously looking up the road for her as she crossed the tracks, with a little box of hot beaten biscuits, cold chicken and pound cake for her lunch. She had sat up half the night preparing it. Ezra Brownleigh, too, hobbled down five minutes before the north bound train to wish her Godspeed. Three minutes later a noisy troop of little girls and one boy whom she had taught music, came plunging down the street, their arms full of big bunches of blue violets and golden buttercups which they pressed upon her. The boy had a big red apple and a very small toad in a match box which he offered her for company on the way. She made him eat the apple himself and told him to take care of the toad for her till she returned. Then the train came whistling down the track, the girls smothered her with moist kisses, Miss Sallie Gibbons folded her in her arms and wept in her neck, and Ezra Brownleigh tried to smile with the tears rolling down his cheeks. She was gone, out into the great wide world of the North! Out to earn her living and win her way. Out toward the end somewhere, which is Eternity!

CHAPTER II

Judson Granniss had always been a lonely boy.

From his birth his mother had tried to dominate him, as she had always dominated his father. She spent her time in shooing him away from almost everything he wanted to do or think or be. And much of the time she succeeded, because he had inherited from his father a gentle, kindly, unselfish nature. But because he was also her child and had as strong a will as hers, there were times when he became like adamant, and then there was war between them.

Strangely enough at such times Judson reminded her of her dead husband whose gentle kindly nature had yielded to her will except on rare occasions when the matter at issue concerned some one else, and then he too became adamant.

Judson's father was a dreamer, by nature an inventor, who had by stern integrity and patient perseverance added to a small inheritance until in the small country town where they had lived when Judson was a child, he had become a power. Then one day he loaned a large sum of money to an old school mate, Jake Dillon by name, who came to him with a tale of a fortune in jeopardy and a motherless child. For the sake of the motherless child Joe Granniss loaned him enough money to set him upon his feet. Jake Dillon became a rich man, and Joe Granniss died a very poor one, because he had trusted his old friend and had loaned the money without security. His wife Harriet never gave him another hour's peace while he lived after she learned of the transaction, and it is to be supposed that she also spent time on Jake Dillon,—and he certainly deserved anything he got,—for Harriet was not the woman to leave her duty toward her fellow man's sins undone.

Joe Granniss closed his kindly thin lips and lived the remainder of his chastened days with very few words, and a wearied look on his prematurely aging face. He didn't fall sick but he failed from day to day, and one morning he didn't get up.

Harriet prodded him because she didn't believe in a grown man giving up to illness, but he only smiled sadly at her, and as the days went by she grew alarmed and hurried around to get a will out of him. She, who had ruled his will all her life, must needs supplicate at the last for the will she had tried to crush. Yet she couldn't manage it after all to get everything put in her name. He *would* leave five thousand from the pittance he had remaining to Judson. The mother couldn't budge him from that. He didn't argue. He didn't even talk. Just shook his head and said, "Jud must have something all his own." Finally she succeeded in tying that up so that Judson couldn't have it until he was thirty if he married before that time without her consent. The dear man must have been almost over the border or he would have foreseen what that would mean to Judson, but he finally assented, and soon after the signing of the will, closed his dreamer's eyes and died.

As he lay there with the dignity of death upon him he seemed so suddenly young again, like one who sees a vision at last and is hastening after, that Harriet in her sudden grief, grew half impatient with him even in death. What right had he to look like that when she was left here on earth to slave alone without him? It was just like him to leave her like that, most of the money gone, and he look *glad*, actually *glad in death!*

Judson Granniss remembered keenly those first days after his father's death. He felt so alone, so utterly desolate. For they two, his father and himself, had come to be a sort of close corporation, allied against the mother. Not that there had been any outward hostilities. She was the Captain and they both did what she said, with a kind of age-old courtesy, a sort of gallantry, because she was a woman, and a wife, and mother, their wife and mother. The old time courtesy had been as much toward the wifehood and motherhood as toward the woman herself. They had quietly, without voicing it, each recognized that the other had things to bear. They loved her but she made them bear a great deal. She lashed them with her tongue unmercifully, sometimes unjustly; yet they were loyal to her. In all matters not absolutely vital to them they yielded, and sometimes when Judson's indignant young eyes would plead with his father to have his own way about going off with the boys for a school game, or something of that sort, the father would say: "She's the only mother you've got, Jud, you know," and Jud's face would relax, and a look of surrender come into his eyes, though one could see his very soul was rebelling.

It was on one occasion like this that the father, watching his boy closely, had suddenly roused with a determined look and said to his wife sharply:

"No, Harriet. It isn't right. He's a boy. You must let him go. He'll never be a man if you coddle him so. Go, Judson. I've said it!" And Judson with a quick wondering glance at his firm father and astonished mother, went, before another word could be said. Whatever his father said to his mother after he was gone, he never knew, but never again did she try to keep him away from the games among the boys, and he grew to be a giant among them in achievements.

Judson could remember in those first days after his father's death, that his mother wrote long letters to Jake Dillon. Angry letters they must have been summoning him to audience. Twice he came. Harriet sent her son to bed, but Jake Dillon talked in a loud raucous voice, a swaggering, braggety voice. Jud couldn't help hearing some things he said. He didn't understand altogether about it, but he gathered that Jake Dillon maintained that he owed his friend Granniss nothing. It was a chance they both took. He had won and Granniss had lost. That was all. Nevertheless Harriet extracted money from him on both occasions, and when he died he left a strange will with life provision for Harriet, and a home with his daughter Emily, provided Harriet would consent to be Emily's companion and look after her comfort. If Emily died first the house and property were to go to Harriet. The will caused a great uproar among the Dillon cousins. They tried to stir up Emily to break the will, but Emily was a peaceable, gentle soul, with a strong sense of justice, and she may have had her own reasons for thinking her father did right in making tardy amends to the family of one of his victims.

Judson Granniss was a mere boy when Jake Dillon died and Harriet prepared to leave their country home in Mercer and move to the Dillon house in a suburb of the neighboring city.

Emily Dillon was an utter stranger to them both and Jud balked with all his father's gentle strength at the move, but Harriet was firm, and they went. The boy wore a hard belligerence in his eyes that first day, and barely spoke to their new house mate, but it did not take him long to perceive that Emily Dillon liked the invasion as little as he enjoyed coming, and in her gentle quiet way was holding them aloof. As the days went by, her smile turned wistfully to his gruff reticence, and gradually they grew to like one another, and almost without words, or even outward sign, to make common cause together in bearing the tyranny of Harriet Granniss.

Emily Dillon was kind to the boy, bought him surreptitious candy, did little things for his comfort when his mother was out at some town function, or on a shopping orgy, even bought a modest automobile for his use as he grew older, which she never learned to drive herself although it was tacitly known as her car. Harriet ruled that as well as everything else in the house, and drove hither and yon whenever she could get Judson out of working hours, and Emily only got an occasional ride now and then. But Emily went on her quiet repressed way growing sweeter and more gentle as the years went by. Judson often wondered why she bore it all. Why she didn't send them away, take some law action or other, or even go away herself. She had money enough herself without the house. Sometimes he reasoned with his mother that she ought to be the one to go, but she only shut her large lips stubbornly, and drew her brows into an angry frown, and told him he was a poor fool who didn't know what he was talking about. Sometimes he thought that when he was a little older he would talk to Emily Dillon about it and try to do something to help her get away from the situation, which he could see plainly would never have been of her choosing; but the time had never yet seemed to come. He sometimes meditated going away himself as he grew older for he felt as if he was an intruder in this woman's home, but whenever he contemplated this some little incident would show him that Emily Dillon was really fond of him, and would miss him if he went; that his presence was really a comfort to her in a situation that would otherwise have been to her well nigh intolerable. He could not help seeing that his mother was hard and intolerant, and yet beneath it all there was a kind of allegiance to her in his heart, the feeling that he was her natural protector. And if he had failed in this feeling there would have been always the memory of his father's old words in his childhood: "She's the only mother you've got, you know, Jud" that would somehow soften his belligerence.

But it was when Judson grew into young manhood, had finished school and gone to work, that his mother's solicitude annoyed him most. He had reached the "girl" stage of most young men, and his mother couldn't understand why he didn't develop a normal interest in them. His shy retiring nature had held aloof from girls while he was in school. He did not like their airs and artificiality. Somewhere in his strong quiet nature was hidden a deep respect and worship for true womanhood. He held an old fashioned high ideal of woman which entirely protected him from any interest in modern girls.

But Harriet would not have it so. Son of hers must go the gait of an ordinary young man. If he did not take to social life naturally he must be made to. That was what she was his mother for. So she undertook to engineer him into society with the result that she found her hands full.

She began by inviting a surprise party for him on his birthday while he was still in high school.

Judson was sitting at the dining room table studying algebra when they came down upon him, and he rose in anger and bewilderment and glared at them as they surged into the room giggling and shouting to one another. They were not particularly interested in Judson Granniss. They considered him dull. But they were always interested in a gathering of their clans with cake and ice cream and a good time generally.

Harriet Granniss had not been modest in her invitations nor discriminating. She had invited the young people in her son's class who attended the high school dances, and added a few from the list of a select private school whose parents were wealthy and influential. She had hired a victrola, and prepared a startling array of cake and sandwiches and salad, and the stage was set for a successful affair, but from the start her son's attitude was hostile. He regarded his party as an invasion, and stood glaring at them until his mother had to call him to account. Whereupon he gravely saluted them all, watched them helplessly through the evening of gaiety as he would have stood by at a gathering of his mother's Aid Society, ready to render aid, but not to participate. He could not dance and he would not try to learn, though the bob-haired Boggs girl was all too eager to teach him. He finally retreated to the kitchen to help with the ice cream and cake. Harriet Granniss' party was a great success, but Judson got no further into society than he had been before. When they were all done giggling their thanks to the mother, and had said a perfunctory good night to the stern young host, his mother turned upon him angrily, and poured a torrent of abuse and advice upon his unbowed head. He listened to her all the way through, with lifted chin and almost haughty look in his gray eyes, and when she was done he said:

"You've made a big mistake, Mother. I'm sorry to disappoint you if that's what you want, but they're not my kind, and I don't want them, nor they don't want me."

Then he turned and went quietly up to his room and his mother was left alone to "tread the banquet hall deserted" and reflect upon her failure. She bitterly charged it to his strange nature inherited from his unfortunate father, "the mistake of her youth" as she phrased it.

But Harriet Granniss did not give up. She never gave up any thing. He was her son and he must be made to go the way of men. Her only mistake had been that she hadn't begun sooner. So she took to scraping acquaintance with girls and inviting them home to see her. Jud would come home from his work and find to his dismay a smiling maiden seated in the parlor and a festive air about the dining room, and he would be sent with unwilling feet to change into his best suit. More reluctant feet would carry him back to the down stairs regions after his mother had issued the call to dinner three times at least, and he would sit through the meal silent and taciturn and his mother wondered why it was that her son should be so sullen whenever anybody came to the house.

Jud was not naturally disagreeable, but it maddened him to have his mother select girls and fling them at him in this open way. He grew wary, and approached his home at night from the back way, entering cautiously, and absenting himself for a meal whenever he had reason to suspect his mother was meditating another dinner guest, and so there grew between them an irritation that was well nigh to wrecking any kind of an understanding there might have been between such a mother and son. They simply were not built on the same plan and it was impossible for Harriet at least to understand this and make allowance for it. She daily and openly bewailed her fate to have such a son, so taciturn, so unconventional, so stubborn.

Emily tried to put in a little gentle word for him now and then, urging his mother to wait and let him alone, to trust to nature to bring the right companionship, for in truth Emily Dillon did not admire the girls that seemed to interest Harriet Granniss. "Girls with some spirit and a little pep to them" she called them. To Emily Dillon they were often coarse and bold and forward. With their flashy apparel, their cosmetics, their loud voices, their unrestrained conversation and actions, and even in several cases their cigarette smoking, Emily Dillon could not understand how Jud was expected to tolerate them. She had however learned that to argue or oppose was but to set Harriet Granniss like adamant to her purpose, so she went her quiet way, said little, smiled always with polite dignity on whatever guest Harriet presented at the table, and watched Jud with satisfaction. She could not help being glad that he did not "fall" as his mother termed it, for any of the girls she brought to the house. Emily Dillon loved Jud as though he had been a younger brother and she revelled in his fine reserve and splendid strength.

Emily Dillon had been her father's protector and slave as a young girl, because she had promised her dying mother to stay with him and take care of him. Sometimes she had been able to keep him from drinking for months at a time, but she had paid the price of alienation from friends and kindred, and from all the things that a young girl counts dear. She had kept his house and tended him like a child when he was drinking, and disagreeable. She bore with his tyrannies and petty cruelties and loved him in spite of it all, she had submitted to scrimping and going without when she knew he was well able to buy her all she wanted, without a murmur; and she had never failed in her loyalty to him and his wishes, though it had gone hard with her when she suspected that he was being unjust and dishonest with others; and so when at last his death set her free and then she found that his will had laid his bonds upon her once more, and put a woman tyrant over her in his place, she gravely and sweetly submitted, knowing that the justice of God might demand this in restitution. Not for even freedom would she hint to any that her father had not been right in anything. Not for worlds would she leave a just debt of his unpaid. This it seemed was the only way to repay the injustice done to Joe Granniss years agone, and so this she must endure. And, well, what did it matter? Life was not a golden pavement to walk down without a care.

The cousins raged and reasoned; they urged and protested, but she was gently firm. She would carry out her father's will. And she lived her quiet life apart, going about in her own house, yet not in reality its mistress, keeping her reserves in spite of all the grilling that Harriet Granniss gave her, looking back to a few bright days in the past, looking ever forward with golden vision to a time when it all should be over forever.

For Emily Dillon had one bright memory in her life that was like a gorgeous jewel, for which all the rest of her sombre life was like a dull but lovely antique setting, valuable because it held the jewel.

Long ago there had been Nathan Barrett, a big, strong clean-souled clear-eyed youth, who had carried her books home from school, taken her chestnutting, and skating, drawn her on her sled, and brought her red apples and the first violets. They had been very young then, and only the first shy dream of love beginning to dawn in their eyes, when one day, Jake Dillon had insulted the young man and driven him from his door; and there before her father Nate had declared his wish and readiness to marry her when the day came that she could leave her home. Then he had gone away as completely out of her life as if he had never been, but the memory of him had dwelt in her soul like a flame that would not be quenched, and given spring to a step that would otherwise have halted, and brightness to the eyes that would otherwise have been dull with the monotony of the years. She had looked for him to return, confidently hoped to hear from him when her father died and she was free, but the years had gone by and he had not come. Yet the jewel burned in her soul and gave her something to cherish, and she kept her sweet patience, and looked to the great beyond for something everlasting to return out of her own love, something that could not perish and would some day be hers forever. She did not reason it out. She just quietly held its dearness to her soul, along with her faith in God, and her hope in Christ, and her love of her mother. Having these she somehow managed to bear the little every day trivialities and look beyond. It gave her a quiet assurance, and a gentle sweetness that Harriet Granniss could not penetrate, could not understand; it was the something about her housemate that nettled her beyond all power of control sometimes. She could not stir Emily Dillon beyond a certain point. In many ways Emily was like Harriet's stubborn son. She called it stupidity. She held them to blame for it, and she nagged them all the more.

Sometimes she caught a look in Emily Dillon's eyes as if she felt *sorry for her,* and that was most maddening of all. *Sorry* for *her! Why,* should Emily Dillon be sorry for *her?* Poor simple minded Emily, who didn't even know enough to be angry that she had to divide her house with a stranger!

Then there were times when Harriet felt almost jealous at the smile that came in Jud's eyes when he answered Emily. Jud was so unnecessarily polite and formal with Emily Dillon, almost as if he thought he hadn't a perfect right in that house. Almost as if it were entirely Emily's house and he a visitor.

Jud spent a great deal of time studying evenings when he ought to have been out having a good time like other young folks. One was only young once and Harriet wanted a son she could be proud of, a handsome dashing fellow with a speedy automobile and many girls following after him. She wanted him to be popular. With all her fierce determined soul she wanted him to be popular. And she had it against Emily Dillon that she encouraged him to stay at home and study. Sometimes he even went to her special own sitting room and read things to her. He never read to his mother. He knew she would only sneer at him, and tell him not to waste his time on such things now, to wait until he was an old man for that; but she felt it in her heart that he went to Emily for sympathy.

So, they lived at cross purposes, those three, whom life had strangely joined in one house, and none of them quite understood the others. One would have known, even as early as that summer that Ariel came north, that something was bound to happen to disrupt a household like that.

CHAPTER III

THE STIR and bustle of the passengers preparing to leave the car roused Ariel from the deep sleep into which she had fallen as soon as the train left Washington.

She rubbed her eyes and looked around in bewilderment, realizing that they must have arrived in Philadelphia, and here was she, but half awake. She passed her hands over her dazed eyes, smoothed back her dishevelled hair, and straightened her hat. Stumbling to her feet she grasped for her satchel in the rack overhead and followed the other passengers up the long platform to the station. She gazed about her in dismay. There seemed so many people, so many, many trains. Her heart beat with almost frightened rhythm, and now that she was here she shrank inexpressibly from what might be before her. She seemed to be suddenly stripped of any preparation which her heart might have made for the coming interview. It became in a flash so important whether they liked her or not.

She was not surprised that there was nobody at the gate to meet her. It was four hours later than she had promised to come, for the train which had brought her from home to the junction had had engine trouble and missed the morning train from the Junction to Washington. There had been three hours to wait and another delay in Washington. It seemed that she had been travelling forever. But she had the address of the library, and had been told to come straight there in case Miss Larrabee failed to meet her. Also she knew Miss Larrabee's home address.

The station was so big it bewildered her, but she saw a large friendly sign "INFORMATION" and went shyly over to the counter to find out how to proceed.

It frightened her to try to get into the trolley cars. They seemed so big and indifferent, and their doors were in such uncertain places. She let several go by while she watched how others did it before she ventured herself.

The way to the library seemed through a maze of traffic. She felt frightened again at the thought of getting out. But when she reached the place and entered the big leather doors into a sort of super-quiet her courage came again and she marched up to the girl behind the big desk and asked for Miss Larrabee:

"She isn't here," answered the other girl, "She's gone."

"Gone?" echoed Ariel. "Do you mean she's gone to the station to meet me? I looked all about where she told me she would be and I didn't see her. It's too bad if I kept her waiting so long. My train was very late—"

"Oh, no," said the assistant librarian crisply as if she couldn't waste the time, "She's *gone*. Not here any more. *Gone home!*"

"You don't mean—Not *Dead?*" said Ariel, wide eyed with awe. Such phrases were connected with death in her mind.

The librarian laughed.

"Mercy no! I hope not. She simply isn't with us any more. She's resigned. They've appointed a new librarian in her place. She had to go home and take care of her sick mother. She lives away up in Maine somewhere."

Ariel stood still growing white to the lips:

"But I don't understand," she managed to say, "I'm to be her assistant. She wrote me to come today and she was to meet me at Broad Street Station at half past twelve. My train was late—"

"Oh, are *you* the one—?" The girl eyed her keenly with a kind of indifferent interest. "But she wrote you the very next day. I saw the letter. She was very sorry but she told you not to come. You see her mother was taken very sick and her father had just died and she had to go home and stay. She wrote that letter a whole week ago, just as soon as the telegram came."

Ariel suddenly looked around for a chair and sat weakly down looking at the other girl with big appealing eyes.

"I'm sorry," said the girl, "But didn't you get her letter?"

"No, I didn't get the letter," said Ariel with white trembling lips, "I—No, I didn't get any letter."

"You look tired, can't I get you a drink of water?" asked the girl. She hurried away with a glass and in a moment was back.

Ariel sat staring ahead, but she took the glass and sipped a few drops. The Custer courage was coming to the front.

"Can I do anything for you?" asked the girl, "It must be annoying not to have understood."

"Thank you," said Ariel handing back the glass and rising, "I think I shall have to go now. Could you tell me where I could find the new Librarian?"

"No," said the other, "She hasn't reached the city yet. She's coming down from New York tomorrow, but it won't be any use for you to see her. She's bringing her daughter with her to assist her. She's a relative of one of the Board of Directors, and they really made this place for her and her daughter I suppose, though you needn't say I said so. I'm not to stay either. I'm only here till they arrive. It's really tough on you, but you'll probably find another job soon. It really isn't Miss Larrabee's fault, for as I told you I saw her writing the letter. It must be the mails. Things often get lost in the mails. Or perhaps in her hurry she forgot to mail it—"

But Ariel with a wan smile had thanked her and was walking away, her little head held high, her sunny eyes clouded with trouble; but her lips brave as ever.

The other girl looked after her anxiously, but there seemed nothing she could do so she went back to the novel she was reading.

Out in the broad strange street Ariel attempted to find a car back to the station. There at least she would have a right to sit down and think, and recover from the blow she had received. Here she felt that she could not quite take it in, it was so sudden and so sharp a reversal of things.

During the long car ride back to the station she found herself saying softly in her heart:

"Dear Lord, are you there? Dear Lord, are you there? You said you'd go with me, are you surely there?"

She got out of the trolley too soon, it appeared, and must walk a block and cross an awful street, so much worse than when she was there before because of the lateness of the hour. There were throngs everywhere, jostling and seeming to know just when to dash in between taxis and trolleys and automobiles. She stood a long time uncertain, trying to make out which way the traffic signs read and whether the policeman in the middle of the road really meant her to come when he held up his hand, and then she made a wild dash. It was not that she was stupid, only tired and dazed, and out of her sheltered life, she had never experienced the noise and crush of the hour and place.

It was only a man on a bicycle who knocked her own. The big truck had stopped and two automobiles had stopped when they saw her coming for somehow there was something delicate and lovely and appealing about Ariel, something alien to the city in her plain country garb, that made people take care of her. The man on the bicycle was head down going like a rocket, and Ariel didn't see him till he was upon her. Then he only grazed her slightly, just enough to throw her off her balance and down upon her knees, and himself full length upon the road.

The traffic officer roared at everybody, swung his sign around to "STOP" and bore down upon them. Some one extricated the man and the bicycle, and kind strong hands lifted Ariel to her feet again. She found herself wondering if it was the Lord, or one of His angels. A man picked up the satchel, all burst open with her little white garments flung about the street, but Ariel was too shaken and dazed to realize. Her face was flaming with mortification.

"Can you walk?" roared the traffic officer.

"Oh, yes, I think so," gasped Ariel trying to smile, and wishing only to get away out of this throng to hide her mortification. To think she should have fallen in the street, and all her own fault the officer had said. He spoke so rudely to her. She was glad her grandmother could not know. He had asked her if she hadn't seen his sign, and told her all women walked along with their heads down and expected to hold up traffic for half an hour while they meandered across the street. He had scolded her like a naughty child! And there were tears in her eyes. She must not cry in the street with all those people looking. And that was her satchel all broken open, and her tooth brush lying in the road. She could never use it again. And people seeing—! It was awful. Would she ever get away? Would they never get her little things picked up? And how was she to carry them now, with the handle off her bag and a great gash in its side?

The young man who was picking up her things gathered her satchel under his arm. He was big and strong and he put a hand under her sore shaken little arm and guided her across to the sidewalk. She was beginning to feel the jar of the fall. Her knee was bruised, and her wrist hurt. Her head was throbbing and little black specks darted before her eyes. She couldn't somehow think. The young man seemed to know how it was for he kept hold of her arm and guided her toward the door of the station.

"Were you going in here?" he asked, and she tried to answer sanely, although she couldn't remember afterward what she had said.

He guided her toward the elevator, and got her up to the waiting room into a seat before he spoke again.

"Do you feel all right now," he asked from what seemed a long way off, "or would you like me to get you a doctor?"

"Oh, no," she said rousing at that, "No, I'm all right. I'm just trembling a little yet—," but her voice trailed off and she put her head back and closed her eyes.

The young man summoned a porter and sent for some aromatic ammonia. In a moment more a glass was at her lips, and she swallowed the dose and then she did sit up and open her eyes, and the color came slowly creeping back into her face.

"I'm so sorry to have made you so much trouble," she said in her soft pleasant southern voice, "I don't know what made me do like this—"

"You had enough to take anybody's nerve. Are you sure you are all right now?"

"Yes, thank you." She smiled and the man knew that here was a girl he could respect.

He smiled back a big warm gentle smile that made her feel he was her friend, yet presumed nothing. She was a southern girl, used to hospitality, used to trusting people. A girl who had been sheltered phenomenally, and was not alert to evil. He saw that she trusted him as a gentleman, and he felt a great yearning to protect her. She in her turn felt that he was the one whom the Lord had sent to guard her.

The young man turned his attention to the dilapidated satchel which he had deposited on the seat beside the girl.

"I'll just tie this up so it will be safe to travel," he said in a matter of fact way, spreading out the newspaper that was in his pocket and wrapping it around the broken, bulging leather bag.

"Oh, please don't take all that trouble," said the girl, "It was an old thing. I'll have to get a new one."

"Time enough for that tomorrow when you've rested

up from the shock," said the man pleasantly. He was deftly folding the paper, and tying it with a string he fished out of another pocket.

"I guess this will do for tonight," he said pleasantly. "Wait, I'll see if they have a handle at the news stand."

He came back in a moment with a wooden handle which he secured to one side of the bundle, and the girl roused from her exhaustion and thanked him with a smile:

"I'm sure I don't know what I should have done if you hadn't helped me," she said, "I think I was bewildered."

"Oh, someone else would have been there if I hadn't" said the young man gallantly, "No one would leave a lady in the middle of the street."

"Not every one would take so much time and trouble as you have I'm sure. And besides, I think you saved me from being taken to the hospital. I think I heard that policeman say something about calling an ambulance, and I shouldn't have liked that."

"Well, I'm very glad if I've helped any. And now what can I do more for you? Shall I put you on your train? Or is there a friend with a car whom I can call up for you?"

"No, thank you," said Ariel rousing to her situation, "I haven't any train, nor any friend. I'm—That is, I don't know—Well, I'm not sure just what I'm going to do. I've got to think. I'll just sit here a little while and get rested I think."

The young man frowned.

"I don't like to leave you here alone till I'm sure you're all right," he said "I'm not so sure you oughtn't go to the hospital and let the doctor give you something. You had a hard fall. You must be bruised."

"Oh, I'm quite all right thank you," she said with a wan little smile, but something in the whiteness of her cheek, the languor of her eye made him loath to leave her thus.

"You ought to have something hot to drink right away," he said suddenly, "Here, come this way."

He picked up the satchel and assisted her to her feet:

"Yes," she said as if the suggestion were welcome, "But I don't need to trouble you any further. Just show me where the restaurant is. I can walk quite well alone now."

He took her arm firmly and guided her through a crowd of people who were hurrying to catch a train, and toward the leather doors of the dining room:

"You're not troubling me," he said cheerily, "I'm tremendously hungry myself. I had a hard day and scarcely any time for lunch. If you don't mind I'll take a bite myself, and then I can see if you're able to be left to yourself."

He seated her at a little white table and summoned a waiter. Ariel looked around anxiously at the palm decked room and deft waiters. A meal in a place like this would cost more than she ought to afford from her scanty store, but what could she do? The man was very kind, and quite matter of fact. He had not taken advantage of her situation in the least. Well, she needed the food, and perhaps she might venture to ask this gentleman a few questions.

The young man gave an order and then turned back to her.

"He's bringing you the tea at once," he said pleasantly, "but I'm getting a steak for myself and they're always too big for one. You'll eat a little of it I'm sure, and then you'll be more fitted to decide what to do. Here comes the tea now."

The hot tea brought the color to Ariel's white cheeks. As the young man watched the life come back into her face with satisfaction he smiled:

"Now," said he, leaning across the table with a confidential tone, "My name is Granniss and I live in Glenside, ten miles out. I wish you'd just consider that I'm your brother for a few minutes and tell me how I can serve you. I don't see leaving you here to sit in the station indefinitely after a fall like that. You ought to be put to bed, and have some one to look after you. If you haven't a train, you must live in the city, and if you haven't a friend won't you just consider me that until you get to your home? I can easily call a cab and see you to your boarding place, or take you in the trolley car if you insist on that, but you ought to be looked after and I'm going to do it until someone else better fitted turns up. Now, tell me please where you are staying?"

CHAPTER IV

THERE was something grave and reassuring about the young man's voice which made her trust him. She wondered if she ought to tell him her situation? It was against all her upbringing and principles to confide her troubles to a stranger, especially a man, and a young one; yet she sorely needed advice, and she needn't take it if she didn't like it.

"You're very kind, Mr. Granniss," she said at length in a quaintly formal tone. "But I'm not staying anywhere. I've just come today. I'm Miss Custer of Virginia—" there was something in the sweet dignity with which she spoke the name that demanded respect. It seemed to summon the long line of noble Custers to speak for her in this informal introduction.

The color swept into Jud's face, and for a moment he felt almost as if he had presumed, yet it was not anything in her tone or manner that made him feel she looked down upon him. It was perhaps the little lifting of her head, patrician born, that made him feel somehow her fineness. He almost wondered at himself for speaking so freely with her. He who had always held aloof from girls.

"I came up to take a position in a library that a friend had, I *thought,* secured for me, but when I reached here I found the friend had been suddenly called far away to care for a sick mother, and had resigned her position.

The letter she wrote me telling me not to come did not reach me, and I find someone else has the position. So you see my plans are somewhat upset. I was absorbed in the perplexity of what I should do next when I was crossing that street or I probably would not have done such a foolish thing as to be run over by a bicycle, and make all this trouble."

"Say, that's tough luck!" said Jud all interest again, "What are you going to do? Have you a place to stop tonight?"

"No," said Ariel, quite composed now and self-possessed, "and perhaps you can advise me, since you're so kind as to offer. I was to stay with my friend, but I haven't an idea where, as I was to meet her at the station, or come to the library if we missed each other. But I've read about the Y.W.C.A. Is there one near here?"

Jud's face lightened:

"There is, of course," he said briskly, "And there's such a thing as a Traveller's Aid Agent right here in the station. If I am not mistaken a friend of some one I know is on duty in the evening here. She would know where was the best place for you to go and you could talk to her all about your problems. That's what she's here for. Just excuse me a minute and I'll see if she's at her desk."

Granniss hurried through the swinging doors and Ariel sat alone, feeling suddenly forlorn in a strange world. Suspicious too, a little, now that he was out of her sight, of the stranger who seemed so determined to help her. She had been so earnestly warned before she left home that she was inclined almost to run away while he was gone, and so be free from him. Yet her innate courtesy would not let her do so in spite of her fears. He had been too kind to treat so shabbily.

Granniss was back in a short time just as the waiter arrived with a well laden tray:

"Yes, Miss Darcy's here," he said in a relieved tone, "I spoke to her about you and she says there's a nice room vacant in a Girl's Club tonight, just for the night, that you can take. The new occupant comes tomorrow. Then tomorrow Miss Darcy thinks she can find something for you more permanent if you want it. She's coming in as soon as she meets a girl on the New York train and sends her to her friends. You'll like her and she will advise you about anything. You know about the Traveller's Aid don't you?"

Ariel shook her head.

"Why it's an organization to take care of travellers, especially women and young girls, who are alone, and don't know where to go or how to find their friends. There is always someone on duty day and night at all big railroad stations to help those who need them. They wear a badge like a policeman's with Travellers's Aid on it, and they have a desk in the women's Waiting Room. There are notices here and there, about, in several languages, telling where to find the Agent, and bearing a facsimile of the badge so strangers or ignorant foreigners will not be afraid to trust her."

Ariel's eyes were dreamy with thought:

"That is wonderful," she said, an almost startled look in her face.

"A pretty good system," said Granniss, "I don't know that it's especially wonderful. It's the right thing. It ought to have been done years before it was."

"Yes, but—well you don't understand—" smiled the girl, "It's a little private wonder all to myself this time. You see I was just a little frightened over coming away from home all alone for the first time in my life, and last night I found a verse in my grandmother's Bible that said 'Fear thou not for I am with thee' and somehow all along the way I've had that proved to me again and again. First there were some friends at the station this morning who planned for my comfort; and then there was you who picked me up, and now there is this Agent. I'm beginning to think God has His agents posted all the way ahead where I have to go, for so far one has met me at every turn of the way."

Granniss looked at the young girl across from him as if she had been a creature from another world:

"Do you really believe that, that God is like that? Caring for people in little things?"

"Why, surely," said Ariel lifting clear eyes without a shade of doubt to his questioning ones, "Don't you?"

He searched her face for a long instant before he answered:

"If I did it would make a whole lifetime's difference with me," and there was a wistfulness about his tone that struck deep into the girl's heart.

"I'm sorry you don't," said the girl simply, "I don't know what I'd do without Him. I've always known He was that way. It isn't just that I believe it's so, I *know* it's so. Why, He's *taken care of me!*"

The leather doors swung open and a little woman with hair tinged with gray under a small black hat and wearing a shining silver badge entered, stood an instant taking a keen survey of the room, then came swiftly to their table. Judson Granniss arose with a quick deference, and drew back a chair for her:

"Miss Darcy, this is Miss Custer," he said and Ariel liked the easy gravity of his speech.

Miss Darcy gave Ariel one swift searching glance and smiled with a softening of the lines of eyes and mouth:

"Judson says you need my help, dear," she said crisply and sat down.

"Now you'll take a cup of tea with us," said Granniss, "Or would you rather have coffee?"

"Just a little tea if you have it there, Jud, I mustn't stay but a minute. There's another train coming in shortly now and I'm due outside. I just wanted to make sure what this little girl needed."

She turned to Ariel and asked a few questions:

"Well," she said when she was satisfied, "I have to meet the eight thirty-five and take a girl to Fifty-second Street. Suppose you wait and go with me. We'll take a taxi and I can leave you at the Club and introduce you so you won't have any more trouble. Jud, you're going-home on the eight five I suppose? Well, you bring her in to my desk and she can sit there till I come if I'm away. Sorry I have to keep you waiting dear. You look as if you needed a good night's rest, but it won't be long now. You sure you don't need to see a doctor? Any bad bruises do you think? You'll feel stiff and sore in the morning likely. Better rest late. Meantime, Jud, you say you heard of a position she might be able to get. Suppose you phone me in the morning, and I'll show her the way before I go out home. Here's my morning number. Say about eight o'clock if you can find out so early in the morning."

"I may be able to see the man tonight," said Granniss.

"So much the better. You can reach me here after half past nine."

Miss Darcy vanished and the man and girl finished their repast slowly. It did not seem to them that they were new acquaintances, and now that the agent had given a sort of background to their introduction Ariel felt much better about their irregular meeting.

It was evident that the young man was in no hurry to conclude the little meal. He sat watching Ariel for a minute or two, almost as if he were not hearing the eager thanks she was uttering.

"Do you know," he said leaning over a bit toward her and speaking in that low confidential tone again, "I'm awfully interested in what you said a while ago. You're somehow different from any girl I ever met before. I wish you'd tell me what makes you so sure you are being taken care of by God. It's always seemed to me He didn't care a hang what became of us all, if there is any God."

"Oh, please don't speak that way," said Ariel, as if his words had hurt her, "It's just because you don't know Him. I'm sure it is. You couldn't be uncertain about it if you did. Why, He's my best Friend, my Saviour, my Guide, my Companion. I'm certain because I *know Him* that's all. It's just like knowing people, only more so. And there isn't any other way to find out but just to get to know Him."

Granniss looked puzzled, hopeless, as if her words meant nothing to him; as if she were a mere child babbling. There was a tinge of disappointment in his eagerness, as if he saw from her words that after all it was just as he expected, a matter of tradition, stock phrases that she had been taught, nothing experimentally practical.

"How could one get to know a God, a Supreme Being away off in His heaven? How *could* one know?"

"Why, of course it's a spiritual thing," said Ariel gravely, " 'God is a Spirit and they that worship Him must worship Him in spirit and in truth.' It isn't a material thing. But then so are our earthly friendships: You can't take hold of what it is that makes us care for one another. It's something outside the flesh. We can express some of it with a smile, a glance of the eye, but friendship is beyond that, it is deeper, more intangible—spiritual. It is how we tell our mother loves us even when she is not near to help us. We are sure because we've tried her. We have known her love. We've tested it. We've been one with her in our daily life. My father used to say there was really only one way to get rid of doubts about God and that was the Bible way, 'He that doeth His will shall know of the doctrine whether it be of God,' just take Him at His word and do His will you know, and try Him. Put Him to the test."

The young man looked at her as if she spoke a foreign tongue.

"You mean to say that by doing certain things you come to know an invisible Being?"

"Doing his will. Trying to please Him. Isn't that the way we get to know other people? Study what they like, be much in their company, do what they want us to do? Isn't that a test of even an earthly friendship, whether we are willing to do what they want us to do?"

"But how could you possibly know what God wanted you to do? I should say that was beating round the bush. That would be as impossible as knowing Him."

"Why, it's all written down in His Book. He's told us there everything He wants. He told us to search it, to know it by heart, to have it on our tongues that we might observe to do it, because it was the way of Eternal Life."

"Do you mean to say that you still believe in the Bible?"

"Oh, of course," said Ariel, "one has to if he wants to

know God. There isn't any other way to find out His will. Of course I know the world is trying to prove that the Bible is just like any other book, but that is so silly to one who knows it, and has found God through it. It wouldn't make any difference to me how much people tried to prove scientifically that I had never had a mother who loved me. They might bring all the arguments and theories in the world and it wouldn't make any difference, because I *knew* her. I have felt her love. She is mine forever!—But, I'm talking just like a preacher, and—aren't you going to miss your train, Mr. Granniss? I've kept you too long!"

Granniss gave a quick glance at his watch, and exclaimed:

"Yes, I must go. I had no idea the time had gone by so swiftly. I mustn't miss that train for I want to find out about that place for you tonight if I can. But I hope you'll let me call on you when you get located. I'd like to talk more with you about this. I never heard anybody talk this way before. It sounds like the real thing, only it's too good to be true."

He summoned the waiter, gathered up his coat and hat and Ariel's bundle and hurried her out to Miss Darcy's desk. He had only a moment to take his leave, and he found a strange reluctance to go.

"I really want to talk some more about this," he said as he left her. "May I come and see you?"

"Why, surely, if I stay here," she said and flashed him a lovely smile.

"I'll do my best to have you stay here," he said and lifting his hat was gone.

She watched him stride away into the throng of train goers, and suddenly felt very much alone. How well acquainted they had become in a few short hours. How strange that he should have stepped out of the crowds to care for her, when it might have been any one of the others who were passing, who would never have taken a thought but to set her on her feet and hurry away. But he, how kind he had been! She had a conviction that he had been on his way home by an earlier train and had delayed on her account. And now she remembered that she had forgotten to offer to pay her share of the meal. She couldn't quite remember when he had paid the check, they had been talking so earnestly. Her cheeks grew hot over the omission. When she thought of it it was rather awful in her to accept a dinner from an utter stranger. What must he think of her when he got away and thought over the evening! Yet he had said he would come again and she must wait until then—or no, she had his address. She might send it to him, only how did she know how much to send? Well, she could find that out very likely by going to that room for another meal and examining the menu card.

She sat in Miss Darcy's big arm chair and watched the crowds come and go; watched the ladies climbing into the high chairs near by to have their shoes cleaned; watched the tired women with babies in their arms, the giddy ones with too much powder on their noses, the cross men who were waiting for their women folks. It was like a great panorama to her country trained eyes. She had travelled a little with her father and mother while she was quite young, but the last five years had been spent very quietly with her grandmother in the old home, and it almost dazed her to be thus suddenly dropped down into the noise and bustle of city life.

When she remembered that she was a stranger in a strange city without a job or a friend, and only a little over fifty dollars in cash between herself and starvation, she was appalled. Yet she was not alone, for her Lord was with her, and hadn't He proved already that His messengers were all along the way? Sometimes they didn't even seem to know they were His messengers. Who knew but she was sent to tell that young man about knowing God? He had seemed interested. Then, as was her wont to pray about everything at all times, she closed her eyes for a moment and prayed:

"Dear Saviour, help him to see, and understand."

Miss Darcy stood beside her for an instant and watched the sweet tired face with the closed eyes, the loveliness of outline, the purity of expression, and her heart went out to the lonely girl. Then she touched her gently on the shoulder and Ariel opened her eyes and realized that here was another of God's messengers on duty close at hand.

CHAPTER V

Out in the darkness the suburban train sped through the night, stopping at every little station to let off a few late stragglers who did not get home to the evening meal. In the last seat of the last car, with his cap pulled unsociably far over his eyes sat Judson Granniss, going over the occurrences of the evening.

Strange that he should have been the one to pick up that girl! He remembered feeling annoyed when she fell just in front of him for he had been running for his train. He had wanted especially to get that train that he might get at a bit of work he had promised to do for one of the business men in Glenside, going over his accounts for him. It would mean several extra dollars in his pocket and he wanted the money. But he had missed the train and thought nothing about it until now. The accounts and the dollars seemed a small matter beside the evening he had spent.

Now that he thought it over, it all seemed such a foreign experience for him to have, a girl, alone, and he taking her to dinner, and anxious to do it! A stranger and he going out of his way to find out her perplexities when he already had enough of his own! Why hadn't he handed her over to the police or an ambulance and run for his train? Why hadn't he hunted up Miss Darcy at the start and at least got the seven-ten home? Why had he lingered, and even been loath to come away now?

Well, she was a wonderful girl. There was no question

about that. Now here was a girl one could like. Why didn't his mother get hold of a girl like that instead of Helena Boggs? He would like to have his mother meet this girl from Virginia and see what a real girl was like. How he would have liked to be able to say to the girl in her perplexity: "Come home to my mother. She'll make it alright and show you what to do. She'll welcome you and help you." But he couldn't imagine doing such a thing. He let his thoughts fancy for a minute what would have happened if he had attempted to bring home a girl he had picked up in the street for his mother to tend. And she would have known the circumstances almost before they got into the house. Trust his mother for that. She would have extracted it from them by a tortuous method all her own, swift and cruel as death. He could remember the time he brought home a little lost puppy in a storm when he was a small child. Harriet Granniss had held her skirts away and waited only to decide on the social status of the little shivering beast, then she took the tongs and holding him at arms length, thrust him out again into the night and the storm while her pleading son stood helpless before her wrath. He could remember the look of disgust upon her face as she slammed the door. And it would have been the same with Ariel; delicate Ariel with her cameo-face and her star-eyes. She would have been swiftly thrust into the blackness of a dark strange world. Yet his mother was a good church member, a professed follower of that God that Ariel knew; a believer, so she declared, in the Holy Scriptures by which Ariel lived! How could the two things be possible? Both followers of the same Christ, yet with such varying results?

He thought over the assured words of the girl, and into his heart there came a yearning to know a God like the one she owned.

He thought of Emily Dillon. She was another one who believed and read the Bible. He had come upon her reading it at different times through the years, a little timid about being caught at it, yet very true to it and reverent about it. Suddenly he wondered if maybe it was not that which made the difference in her life. He tried to think if there were more he knew who were guided by that Book, but could not be sure of any whom he knew well enough to judge.

He did not go directly home but tried to find the man who wanted to employ someone in his office. He found him at last but only to hear that the position had been filled that morning, and he went home quite disappointed and trying to think how he might help to find Ariel a position. Somehow he could not bear to think of her having to return to Virginia. He wanted to get acquainted with her, to know if she were really as wonderful as she seemed.

Harriet was terribly upset at his late home coming. She had had Helena Boggs to supper, and there was steak and mushrooms she told him; and her voice berated him purringly as she aired her grievances. She was like a hen scolding a chicken. It got on Jud's nerves terribly. He finally went up to his room without telling his mother where he had been, which was an offense he knew he would have to answer for sooner or later. Harriet usually managed to get out of people just what they had done so that she might deal out adequate punishment.

But tonight for some reason her son was not nearly so pregnable as usual. His mind was wholly absorbed in trying to think up a job for Ariel Custer, and all too well he knew his mother's ability to pierce his strongest reticence, so he took himself away to his own room and locked his door.

Poor Harriet. She lay awake and wept her bitter tears about that boy. She never had understood what a wonderful boy he was, nor what a nagging, mistaken, bitter, domineering woman she was; and she probably never would till the great day of Judgment and Understanding revealed it to her; but she suffered intensely in her bitter way in every fibre of her big intolerant soul and body.

So she lay awake and planned for her son's good. Planned how Helena Boggs and she could make him over into the very amiable and pliant Judson Granniss that she had always wanted him to be, and confidently expected him to turn out to be some day, somehow, just because he was her son and she loved him.

In his small iron bed in a tiny hall bedroom in a house not two blocks away Dick Smalley wakened after a restless sleep, and began to plan for Harriet Granniss' good. He figured that she needed a lesson. She had thrown a stone at his dog Stubby and driven him from a perfectly good bone which he had got for him at the market with five cents of his newspaper money. She had taken the bone which the dog had dropped when the stone hit him, and thrown it into her garbage pail! It wasn't her bone! She had no right! He had paid for that bone! Stubby wasn't doing her any harm, just quietly eating it in her back yard to get away from that pest of a terrier that lived next door. He would have gone away if she had told him. He was only a dog. He didn't know she minded. But she didn't tell him to go. He knew for he was delivering a paper at the side door of Harriet Granniss' next door neighbor when it happened. He had hurled himself over the fence leaving his papers behind him on the step, and had told her in youthful though forcible language what he thought of her, "where to get off" he expressed it, and she had turned on him and told him she would report him to the police and tell his mother, and that he was not fit to be delivering papers to decent citizens. "Tell his mother!" He a kid that got up every morning and went out on his route like a man; a kid that the men at the fire house spoke of as a "tough egg." Tell his *mother!* He called a taunt to her that was not fit for orthodox Congregational ears to hear and Harriet slammed her door and retired with a vanquishing air while Stubby yelped down the street with a broken foot mourning a lost bone.

Dick had glared at the kitchen door for a minute, and then with a look that promised future return vaulted the fence, recovered his papers and went wrathfully on his way. But he had not forgotten the episode though the day had been full of others. And if he had been so inclined Stubby would have reminded him. Stubby who was his master's shadow, never losing sight of him from sun up to sundown, now forced to an ignominious cushion with his poor foot in a bandage. Stubby who lay on the foot of his bed tenderly guarded and pampered! Stubby should be avenged!

The dog stirred and whined in his sleep, and the boy tossed and planned, but finally decided that the offending garbage pail should be the medium through which vengeance should be done. The bone should return to the hand that flung it away. So Dick turned over and went to sleep like a cherub with Stubby's well paw held tight in his own grubby one.

Quite early the next morning, while it was yet dark, came a sturdy shadow stealing across the back yards, across the hedges silently, skillfully, until he came within range of Harriet Granniss' garbage pail. Carefully reconnoitreing he managed quite silently to find that bone and tie it to the door knob. Then with a noisy clatter he flung the cover of the pail to the brick pavement, and lifting the pail from its high hook where dogs could not possibly maraud it, he sloshed the contents thoroughly and pervasively across the neat gray floor of the back porch and dropped the pail down the steps with a bump and a bang. An instant later the back window was flung up and Harriet Granniss' head in curlers came forth impressively, but Dicky was far and away down toward the station after his early morning papers by that time, and Harriet's demands to know who was there rang on empty air.

It was still too dark for Harriet Granniss to see the havoc wrought so she withdrew her head and slammed down the window when she discovered her efforts were futile, with the conviction that she had frightened the intruder away. But when at six o'clock she descended the stairs and noisily began her preparations for a virtuous breakfast, she opened the back door to take in the milk, and the whole devastated porch was revealed.

The view of Harriet Granniss' face when she first saw it resembled a large black storm at sea with the lightning playing over it. The blackness lasted through the breakfast hour which began on the usual dot, in spite of the fact that both back porch and garbage pail had been duly scrubbed and were gleaming in their usual freshness. Disapproval sat heavily upon her moist unhappy countenance and Emily Dillon was made somehow to feel as if she were the cause of whatever trouble there was.

Harriet announced the distress toward the close of the meal with her usual fine sarcasm:

"Well, we're beginning to get the benefit of your philanthropy at last, Emily."

Emily lifted sweet dreamy eyes from a plate that was almost as well filled with creamed codfish and potatoes as when it was first passed to her, and smiled pleasantly:

"Yes? How is that?"

It was one of Harriet Granniss' grievances that Emily never called her by her first name. She always avoided calling her at all.

She waited until she had poured Emily's coffee before she answered. She considered it one of her prerogatives to pour the coffee and sit in the seat of mistress, and Emily quietly let her do as she pleased.

"You would buy morning papers of that little rat of a boy that lives up the street. Smalley the name is. His mother is that washed out piece that goes by here Sundays in purple. Well, you ought to have been down here this *morning*"—Harriet spoke as if it were now nearly noon, although it had but just struck eight—"You would have seen how much gratitude the little beast has. He emptied the garbage pail all over the back porch and it was filthy! And there was a great big bone tied to the door knob."

"A bone?" questioned Emily, "Whose bone?"

"Well, I'm sure I didn't stop to identify the bone," snapped Harriet, "I had enough to do to get the mess cleared up before the grocery man came. It wasn't *my* bone, I'm sure of that! It may have been yours, of course if you find one missing."

Harriet considered this grim humor.

"I mean," said Emily smiling gently, "Was it *our* bone?"

"*Our* bone!" repeated Harriet, "I didn't know we had any bone in common, except a bone of contention."

"I *mean*," said Emily again with a worried look, "Did it come from our house? Was it a bone from our table? Our meat you know?"

"Well, no, I don't suppose it was," grudged Harriet, "What difference does that make?"

"Not much, and yet—if it was brought here for that purpose—"

"Well, no, it wasn't brought here for that purpose. If you've got to know the exact ins and outs of it, it was a bone a dog brought here and I threw a stone at him and took his bone away and put it in the garbage pail."

"Oh, I see." Emily ate another bit of fried potato.

"Well, what do you see?" snapped Harriet. But Emily remained silent.

"I gave that dog a lesson he won't forget soon," crowed Harriet, "He went off yelping up the street with one foot in the air. It's ridiculous keeping dogs in a town. They've no business doing it. If I had my way all the dogs would be shot!"

"Oh, poor fellow!" said Emily involuntarily, stooping to sip her coffee.

"Yes, poor fellow! That's you! I suppose you'll be wanting to bring a dog home yourself next! But nobody need try to keep a dog around me! If you'd seen that back porch I had to scrub! But you never think of saying poor Harriet. Yes, I suppose that'll be the next thing I'll have to be called upon to endure. A nasty little mangy dog!"

"Oh, no!" said Emily, "I wouldn't think of it!"

"Well, I'm going to see that boy's mother this morning, and believe me she'll learn a few things about how to bring up children. And if she doesn't do something about making that boy apologize I'll report it to the police. He *ought* to have been made to clean up the mess. I'd have liked to rub his dirty little freckled nose in the garbage, only I didn't want the baker to see it when he came."

"Oh," said Emily aghast, "Please! I wouldn't go to the neighbors about a thing like that! Just let it pass! It won't likely happen again!"

"Yes, let it pass! Let it pass! That's you all over Emily!

No indeed I won't let it pass. This is part my house isn't it? I do the morning work, don't I? Well, I'm *going!*"

With that she gathered her cup and plate and silver and sailed out to the sink with them and Emily beat a hasty retreat to her room to reflect on what she could do to prevent trouble with her neighbors. She was very fond of Dick Smalley's little dog Stubby. She often slipped Stubby a peppermint between the hedge when Harriet was out. She could read a great deal between Harriet's lines, and she decided to slip up to Mrs. Smalley's that morning while Harriet went to market and forestall her. Emily was fond of freckled-faced Dick Smalley. She sometimes gave him smiles when she gave Stubby peppermints.

So Emily put on her neat black hat and coat and slipped away while Harriet went to market.

CHAPTER VI

EMILY stopped at the little candy shop on the corner and bought a few peppermints for Stubby.

She had decided to say she had come to buy three extra copies of the *Ledger* if Dick had any left. This would be a good excuse, and then she could gradually find out if Stubby was hurt, and perhaps get it in to apologize for Harriet's dislike for dogs. She felt she might perhaps be able to extract the sting as it were from anything that Harriet might say about Dick or the dog, supposing Harriet really meant to carry out her threat. She did not really believe that Harriet meant to do what she had threatened.

But when the door was opened to her knock she found a very small little Smalley sister of Dick's at the door knob, and an angry Mrs. Smalley inside talking loudly over the telephone to the chief of police. She discovered to her dismay while she waited that Harriet had preceded her, and had done all and more than she had promised to do at the breakfast table, and that Mrs. Smalley was now planning her revenge.

Mrs. Smalley turned to her caller with fire in her eye, but Emily Dillon's smile was disarming:

"I'm so sorry, Mrs. Smalley," she said, "And so ashamed. Mrs. Granniss is very quick you know, and rather sharp with her tongue sometimes but she really doesn't mean all she says,—"

"Well, she better not," bristled Mrs. Smalley, "I'll have the p'lice on her. Comin' here, makin' a fuss about the kid. He's full o' the devil I know, but he ain't meanin' any harm, an' he never would a touched her garbage pail if she hadn't a stole Stubby's bone that Dicky bought with his own money at the butcher shop. She said our Stubby was trespassin' but you can't always be sure a dog knows his own premises, and anyhow Dicky was only in the next yard a deliverin' papers. An' Stubby wasn't doin' her any harm down under the hedge gnawin' his bone. See him now, poor little soul, a layin' there mournin' fer Dicky 'cause he can't go out. He tries to get up an' limp but his leg's clean broke, an' it'll take days to heal so he'll be the same dog again—"

Emily Dillon was down on her knees beside the little sufferer, petting him and feeding him peppermints, and Mrs. Smalley was soon forgetting her grievances and telling all Stubby's and Dicky's virtues; telling what a hard time she had had to meet the payments on her little bungalow since Smalley died, and how Dicky helped her with the washes she took in, and sold papers, and worked for the grocery man out of school hours; and how Stubby barked for them to let the cat in nights, and wouldn't let a book agent in the gate, and took care of the baby when she was busy; and all the one and another little joys and sorrows of a hard existence from hand to mouth.

Emily Dillon left a five dollar bill to pay a dog doctor

to see Stubby's leg and be sure it was getting on all right, and another whole dollar for Dicky to spend in peppermints; and while she was there called up the policeman and talked to him pleasantly all about the affair, asking him please not to proceed with any action against Mrs Smalley, "For it's really my house you know," she said gently, "Mrs. Granniss is only living with me, and she's terribly afraid of dogs, and rather quick with her tongue."

She was so pleasant about it all that Mrs. Smalley was smiling and thanking her, and before she left she took her into the west bedroom that she said she wanted to rent "if she could get the right party," and Emily Dillon was all interest and promised to search for "the right party;" and so they parted friends.

That was how it came that Emily Dillon knew about the pleasant little west bedroom that was for rent so cheap and looked out on a garden of daffodils and pansies, when Jud told her that night—while his mother was at prayer meeting—about Ariel and her need for a home. Ariel who had not succeeded in getting in at the Y.W. because it was all full, with a long waiting list. Ariel who had not yet found a position and might have to go back to Virginia where there was nothing to do to earn her living and only kind friends who had nothing to lend her.

Emily Dillon watched Jud as he talked and grew thoughtful. Presently she said:

"I'd like to meet her, Jud. I might know of something for her. I heard about a room—" but she did not finish the sentence. She wanted to see Ariel first.

"Why not go in town with me in the morning and meet her? Miss Darcy let her have her room for tonight, and I can take you to the door and introduce you."

"I'll do that, Jud," said Emily with a gleam in her eyes. Jud smiled back. He felt toward Miss Emily almost as if she instead of Harriet were his mother. He had always been in a protective attitude towards his real mother, protective against herself. It was the old reminder of his father, "Jud, she's the only mother you've got," that made him feel as if he must take care of her against herself. His mother just didn't always see things as they were, that was all. But Emily Dillon saw, and she knew enough to keep her tongue still.

Neither of them said a word about the expedition to Harriet Granniss at the breakfast table. Emily came down with her hat on and merely said she found she had an errand in town, and Harriet was always miffed by that. Why on earth couldn't Emily Dillon discuss her affairs openly the way other people did? Harriet Granniss thought it secretive, and it made her downright mad. Besides, she would have gone to town too if she had been asked. But Emily never asked her. She was gentle and polite and kind to her as a house mate but she did not attempt to make her a companion. Emily went her way alone. That was what Harriet resented bitterly.

Jud went out as soon as he had finished his breakfast. He did not wait for Emily. But they met on the station platform with a smile as though it had all been planned out that way. Jud would have liked to walk with Miss Emily from the house, but he knew his mother would be jealous as a cat so he went ahead.

So Emily Dillon met Ariel, and loved her at once.

Ariel was all smiles. She had heard of a job and she was to go to it that day. A man wanted her to look after his office and answer letters. Miss Darcy knew that he was considered all right though rather hard on his help, but she didn't mind that. It was a job. She was only to get ten dollars a week until she had learned short hand, and he would pay her fifteen as soon as she could take dictation.

Jud frowned at that and called it starvation wages, but Ariel laughed and said it was better than nothing, and if anything else better came along she could take it. Now she had only to hunt for a room. They seemed hard to find.

Then suddenly Emily Dillon said gently:

"There is a nice little room in Glenside for three dollars a week. Could you afford that? It would mean car fare of course, but it is very pleasant, looks out on a garden, and you would have the privilege of cooking in the kitchen if you wanted to."

Ariel was delighted, and Emily called up from the station and told Mrs. Smalley to hold the room for that evening, that a young woman, a friend of hers, was coming out to look at it and would probably take it at once. In her turn Mrs. Smalley was duly grateful, and Emily went smiling back to her grumpy house mate and finished the day by helping out in a wild orgy of house-cleaning. When Harriet Granniss was particularly hurt about something she always cleaned house.

Ariel came out on the train with Jud who had promised to show her the way to Smalley's, and as bad fortune would have it Harriet Granniss was just finishing off her day by a vigorous shaking of the front door mat as they passed the house.

"Who was that washed-out looking girl you were with?" she sulkily greeted her son as he came in two minutes late to his supper, with a pleased look in his eyes.

"Miss Custer," said Jud looking uncomfortable.

"Custard?"

"Custer."

"Well, that doesn't tell me a thing."

"What do you want to know Mother?"

"I want to know who she is."

"Well, I've told you. She's Miss Custer. She's employed in the city and she's living out here."

"Where?"

"Why, up the street somewhere; has a room or boards or something," said Jud miserably trying to keep his eyes on his plate and look natural.

"Isn't she the young lady that is stopping with Mrs. Smalley?" asked Emily Dillon pleasantly trying to help him out.

"Mrs. Smalley!" Harriet eyed her son viciously as if he had committed some crime. "Do you mean to say you are going with a young woman who lives with a person like Mrs. Smalley?"

"What's the matter with Mrs. Smalley? I don't know

her from Adam," growled Jud his temper rising. "I'm sure I didn't notice which house it was. It's one of those up there. And I'm not 'going with' anybody. Mother. Is it 'going with' someone to happen to walk up from the station with them?"

"Where did you meet her?" demanded the excited mother.

"What does that matter?" The son was beginning to get his stubborn look on. At such times he bore a fleeting resemblance to his mother.

"Well, I want to know."

"Say, look here, Mother. You've made a great fuss because I didn't have anything to do with girls, and now when I simply walk up from the station with a girl who lives on this same street you are raising the devil."

"Judson Granniss! Things have come to a pretty pass if you have to *swear* at your mother! It shows how far things have gone—"

"Mother!" Jud shoved his chair back sharply and arose.

He faced her with stern eyes, and with stern eyes she faced him back, grim and hard and full of jealous bitter love that was so deep it looked like hate.

After an instant Jud's face softened, and his habitual self-control took command.

"Mother, you are utterly unfair," he said earnestly, "I scarcely know this girl at all, yet because I walk up from the station with her you are making a mountain out of a mole hill. Besides, suppose I knew her better; wouldn't I have a right to walk with her as well as with any girl? You have spent time urging me to go with girls and now the first time I've been seen with one you act like this."

"Yes! *Such* a one!" sneered Harriet. "I might have known after all I've tried to do for you that it would turn out this way. When you do go with a girl you pick out *one like this!*"

She got out an immaculate handkerchief and crumpled it viciously to her eyes.

"What do you *mean*, Mother?" Jud thundered. He was angry now and thoroughly disgusted, "What do you know about Miss Custer? What right have you to talk that way about a girl who is an utter stranger to you?"

"It's enough to know where she lives!" declared Harriet with a toss of her head. "That Smalley woman—"

"That has nothing whatever to do with the girl. She rents a room in a decent respectable neighborhood. She knows nothing whatever about the personal character of her landlady beyond the fact that she has been told she is all right. But I'm sure I don't see why you have it in for poor little Mrs. Smalley. She certainly is a self-respecting woman with a perfectly good character. She's doing her best to earn her living and keep her little home for her children since her husband died."

"Oh, yes, her children! *Brats!* That's what they are! She oughtn't to be allowed to keep them with her, such language as she is teaching them. I guess you don't know what that little brat of a boy did to us. Emptying the garbage pail all over our clean back porch! And such vile talk! I wouldn't soil my lips repeating it. The woman herself isn't far behind her child. You should have heard how she roared at me when I went to see her about it; and the little girl, only a baby, stood behind the door and stuck out her tongue at me all the time I was there, and the mother never said a word to stop her. Oh, yes, she's a perfectly good respectable woman of course, and a girl who would live with a woman like that is better of course than a nice wholesome healthy capable girl like Helena Bo—!"

But Jud had had enough. He shoved his chair fiercely away from the table and left the room with as near a slam of the door as Jud ever let himself give in Emily Dillon's house.

Emily Dillon, by no means relishing the position of witness in a scene like this, swallowed her last sip of coffee and gathered her dishes to make a hasty exit to the kitchen, but Harriet, her eyes streaming with angry tears, her nostrils wide spread like a battle horse, pinioned her with a glance:

"Now, what's the matter with *you?*" she snorted. "You don't have to take offense in a matter like this, get mad and go off without eating your dinner!"

"Indeed," said Emily fluttering back to her place, "I've eaten all I wanted. You've been talking you know."

"Yes, I've been talking. Of course you don't approve of what I said. That would go without saying. You never do. It isn't any business of yours of course, but you go around with your head up—"

"You're mistaken," said Emily, "I had no thought except not to intrude."

"That couldn't be possible," nagged Harriet, who deprived of the rightful prey of her son sought solace in blaming another, "People *have* to think. You *know* that you sided with Jud! You *always* do. I can see it in your face."

"I am not siding with anybody," said Emily evenly, "I'm always sorry for misunderstandings—"

"Misunderstandings! As if this was a misunderstanding! No, it's all too plain. My son is all bound up in that yellow haired girl. He has no eyes for his mother any more. And *you uphold* him in it!"

Emily Dillon was almost at the end of her gentle beat.

"Listen. I'm not upholding anybody—"

"No, you never think it's your duty to uphold *me*, his *mother!* You're never sorry for *me*—"

"Yes, I'm often sorry for you," said Emily rising now as though to conclude the subject, "I think perhaps if you wouldn't be quite so insistent with Judson you would more often get what you want. He's a good boy, but no young man likes to be watched and told what he ought to do—"

Harriet Granniss arose in angry amazement and stared at Emily while she finished this unwonted speech and then with flashing eyes she retaliated:

"Thank you for your advice. As you've been a mother to so many young men and had such great experience in raising families of course your advice must be worth its weight in gold. And of course you know my son's temperament a great deal better than I do. It's a wonder the Lord didn't give him to you instead of to me to raise; but as he didn't I suppose I'll have to rub along and do the best I can by asking your advice. But you can save your sympathy. I don't want it. Nobody on earth knows how to sympathize with a mother whose son is going wrong—" She put up her crisp handkerchief to her eyes, and dabbed them viciously.

"But Jud isn't going wrong," broke forth Emily involuntarily, "Jud's a wonderful boy. Everybody says so. You ought to be proud of him. And don't you think you can trust him to pick out a nice girl? What is the use of all the years you have brought him up if he can't judge character now?"

"There you go again. But of course you're not to be blamed, never having had a son of your own, and never expecting to have. You don't understand that this is only the beginning. If a man falls in love,—or thinks he does, which amounts to the same thing,—with the wrong girl it's all up with him. It's too late. I intend this thing shall be nipped in the bud, and if you can't help me you can at least keep out of it. Anybody can see that girl he was walking with tonight wasn't fit to go with, she's too pretty. Even if she didn't live in a questionable place, she's too good looking. A girl like that *can't* be good in this age of the world, and I don't intend she shall get her claws on him. It's my business to stand between him and all womankind because I'm his mother, and I'm going to do it. If he persists he'll learn that he'll have to choose between her and me, and I flatter myself I've enough hold over my own son—if it came to that—"

"But, suppose—" timidly persisted Emily Dillon, because she felt that this was a strategic time in Jud's life and might mean his life-long happiness or sorrow— "Suppose this is a good girl,—suppose you would like her if you got to know her, and she was the girl God meant for your son. You wouldn't want to interfere with a happy life for your son—"

Harriet put down the dishes she was holding with a thud and put her hands on her hips, her chin out, her brows furious:

"Emily Dillon, will you mind your own business? Who set you up, I should like to know, to tell me what to do, with your supposings and supposings. You think because your father sensibly prevented you from running away with a country lout poor as a church mouse and ruining your life that the worst thing that can come to a person is not to get married. Oh, you didn't know I knew that did you? But I am not so dumb as I seem. Because you're an old maid you're morbid about Love and all that slush. Now, I want you to understand that you can mind your own affairs and keep out of mine hereafter."

With that she swept heavily up stairs to her room and locked her door noisily, spending the rest of the evening in a thorough cleaning out of her clothes closet and bureau drawers, thumping them hard on the floor when she brushed the dust out.

Emily, her cheeks flushed to burning, turned with a humbled droop of her fine little head, and went to the sink where she washed the dishes quietly with a few tears mingled in the dish pan, and left the kitchen as neat as a pin. Then she went up to her room, locked her own door noiselessly, and lay on her bed a long time trying to get steady and calm. After which she knelt in humiliation asking for strength to carry on this tempestuous life that she had been called upon to live. It seemed to her that the very centre of her soul had been taken out and raked and bleeding thrust back again within her throbbing body; and that her innermost secrets had been held up to the ridicule of the world; so had Harriet's cruel taunts tortured her sensitive nature. But after a while she grew calm, and prayed for Jud. Poor patient splendid Jud, and the sweet little girl that had come to live in their street.

CHAPTER VII

MEANWHILE, Ariel, in her little new room looking out on the pansy bed was kneeling by a hard little iron bed and thanking her heavenly Father for this haven of rest.

The room was small, but it was large enough for Ariel's few worldly goods. Her little old trunk filled with her simple wardrobe, half a dozen books and some old photographs were all she had to put away; and the trunk containing them would not come out from the city until the next day.

There was a cretonne curtain with blue and green parrots amid red banana leaves across one corner of the room where she might hang her dresses, and there was a golden oak bureau, two chairs and a little table with a wobbly leg, besides the bed. It was clean enough, and cheery enough for a girl who had spent two nights in city lodgings and she appreciated finding it. Mrs. Smalley said she had a gas hot plate with two burners that she might have on a box in the corner to cook her own breakfasts on if she wanted to. There was a gas attachment where they used to have a little gas heater last winter. She said twenty-five cents a week would be all right for the extra gas, if she wanted to cook, and Ariel saw how she might cut down expenses still more by getting her own meals night and morning and eating a good lunch in the city in the middle of the day.

She opened her bundle and began to put her things away. Miss Darcy had given her a paste board suit box, so her old satchel had been discarded.

Some of her garments were streaked with dust from the street when she had fallen down, and as she brushed them and busied herself wiping out the bureau drawers and lining them with pieces of a newspaper she had brought home with her, her thoughts were busy with the way she had been kept since she had left home. She realized once more vividly how like a miracle it was that she had not been run over by that great truck that towered above her as she fell, or the big blue touring car that came to such a sudden halt above her very head.

Or suppose she had broken her leg or her arm, and had had to go to a hospital and then be unable to work for days and weeks. She certainly had been kept miraculously. Of course she was no exception in the world. Other people were kept too, each human life that went on from day to day was a continual miracle, but she felt the upholding so strongly in her own case because without it she would have been so alone in the world. If anything ever happened to her up here no one would know. There were dear people at home who would care, who might even worry a little about her if they never heard from her, but none of them would or could leave their homes and their business and come up to look after her. If she got sick or died she would simply go out as far as this world was concerned. But she could never go out from God's presence.

Carrying on these deep thoughts she came at last to the young man who had picked her up and been so solicitous for her welfare; to the Traveller's Agent, who had been so kind, and to that dear Miss Dillon who looked so like a little dove. She felt she was going to love Miss Dillon. How nice that she lived nearby. They would often see one another perhaps. Mr. Granniss had pointed out the house where they lived with the hedge about it, as they passed, when he was showing her the way here. She liked Mr. Granniss. He seemed so strong. It would be fine to have a friend like that. He had nice eyes with deep lights in them like the twinkle of the stars in the old well at home when one leaned over the edge of the stone wall and looked down below the oaken bucket. She wished again she might help him to know and love her Bible.

She took it up tenderly, brushed off the dust marks on

the cover, hunted a little white towel that had not been mussed to spread on the table. Then she put the Bible on it, laid her mother's old fashioned gold watch beside it, and drew up the creaking little rocking chair. This was her home, and now with the open Bible it looked more like living.

She turned over the leaves lightly and again the book fell open to Isaiah. It was heavily underlined in a trembling hand. Her grandmother's she knew, and on the margin had been written in fine little letters "Tried and proved." Many a time had her grandmother told her the story of one of God's saints who always wrote that on the margin of a promise that he had put to the test. As she read over the familiar words she felt as if she were walking down the path of her grandmother's garden and seeing all the blossoms that were so dear to her. It seemed so safe and precious to be reading out of grandmother's book words that grandmother had tried and proved. And to know they were for her. Suddenly she searched in her little handbag and got out the tiny gold pencil that used to be her mother's and wrote beside her grandmother's trembling testimony, her own "Tried and proved by Ariel also."

She turned the leaf and began to read the forty-third chapter. More "fear nots." On down through the chapter, verse after verse marked "tried and proved" and set her own initials as she remembered her own leading these last two days.

Suddenly she came to a verse that seemed to break the thread of thought:

"Bring forth the blind people that have eyes, and the deaf that have ears." How queer. What could it mean? Why—was 't that like Mr. Granniss? He had eyes but he couldn't see the goodness of God.

Her eyes dropped down to the tenth verse:

"Ye are my witnesses, saith the Lord, and my servant whom I have chosen; that ye may know and believe me, and understand that I am He—"

It almost seemed as if God, the great God were speaking to her. Could it be that He meant that He had put it into her heart to try to make that young man see what he had not seen before about God? "My witness!" What if she could be God's witness!

Her eyes glanced over at the column just back of where she had been reading:

"And I will bring the blind by a way that they knew not; I will lead them in paths that they have not known: I will make darkness light before them, and crooked things straight. These things will I do unto them, and not forsake them."

Stranger and stranger! Didn't it seem as if the great God were talking it all over and promising her that if she witnessed He would set his seal of success upon her effort and show how true He was? But how would she know what to say? How be sure she would not do harm?

She glanced back again one more column on the next page: "I the Lord have called thee in righteousness, and will hold thine hand, and will keep thee, and give thee for a covenant of the people, for a light of the Gentiles; to open blind eyes, to bring out the prisoners from the prison, and them that sit in darkness out of the prison house. I am the Lord—"

Ariel was not at all sure that she understood whether this might not mean something deep and strange that she did not understand; something pertaining to the Jews and Gentiles perhaps, but surely, surely the Lord was bringing a meaning to her soul. Surely it seemed as if He were asking her to witness for Him to those who were blind to Him, and did not know Him; and that He was promising to go with her and hold her hand.

Very reverently Ariel closed the book and knelt down, her head upon its cover:

"Dear Lord," she prayed, "I don't know whether I have understood aright or not, but if you want me for your witness I'll be glad to do it. I know what you've done for me and I can tell it. But I'm glad you're going to hold my hand, because I might make so many mistakes. Don't let me try to say anything of my own, just your words that you put into my heart to say, and if I am presuming in thinking you mean this, please stop me, and don't let me do any harm in the great wonderful kingdom of God."

Ariel slept sweetly on her little hard bed, but Jud was out on the hillside walking the woods alone, and thrashing his bitter thoughts out with himself. He had no God to commune with, only his own heart thoughts, and sometimes they failed him in time of need, and a great fury rose within him so that he could scarcely contain himself. At such times the woods had for years been his refuge, and tramping for hours neath a curtain of dark he would somehow find his self-control again.

But tonight he seemed to be stirred deeper than usual. The very fountains of his being had been penetrated by his mother's prodding tongue. He felt as if something inside him were bleeding to death, something sweet and good that had just been born, and he did not quite know what to do with himself.

Once he flung himself down on a great rock above a stream and stared up at the sky. The stars seemed so far away. He thought of God, and of what Ariel had said. How could it be possible that God cared? Why had God made him anyway? What was the use of life? Why was his mother the way she was? Why couldn't things all be sweet and good? Why should one have to live if life was to be a continual turmoil, with all things which seemed sweet and good and right trampled under foot?

Was there anything in what Ariel had said—for he had come to call her Ariel in his thoughts now—about putting God to the test? Taking that promise about doing His will? He would ask her more about it when he saw her again. He would like to read the promise himself. He wished he had a Bible, but if he had he wouldn't know how to find it. Of course there was his mother's Bible, but it was beyond thought that he could go to that. She had never brought him up to love her Bible. It was a book of severity to her. The fear of the Lord she held up to him, never the love of the Lord, never the Forgiveness of sins, nor the atoning blood. Christ was a Saviour, but of what she never said. Jud had gathered the hazy belief of the masses from his youthful compulsion at Sunday School, but the private application of such truths as he had absorbed had never appealed to him, so as he grew older he rejected all of it, and pronounced himself an unbeliever. His subsequent studies both at school and in evening classes in the University had tended to strengthen this decision. He had grown to feel that the Bible was for women who didn't know any better. That Miss Emily drew sweet comfort therefrom made him regard the Bible tolerantly, but more from reverence for the reader than for the Book. And if his mother's life was any indication of the Book by which she professed to be guided, then he wanted nothing of it.

He had never met anyone before Ariel who talked about it as she did. It had never occurred to him that there were any young people any where who had an intelligent belief in the Scriptures. And Ariel was intelligent, far beyond the average, he could see that at once. Yet Ariel lived by the Book and loved it, even as Emily Dillon seemed to do, only with a more basic belief. She understood and could tell why she believed. Did Emily Dillon perhaps, have this soul-evidence too? Had she in quiet way put it to the test in her life and found it true?

But Emily Dillon seldom talked. Perhaps her belief was more intelligent after all than one knew. What if after all God cared? But how could He care and let such things be as what happened tonight at dinner? How could He let terrible disasters and troubles come upon the people that He loved—if He loved them? The old round of questions that the devil propounds whenever a straying soul seeks to find the truth.

Gradually the night and the quiet calmed Jud's soul, and something of the Infinite all about him made him long inexpressibly to cry out to God about it, just to ask Him why if He loved him He didn't do something about the state of things in his life? Why He didn't speak out plainly and let him know what was the truth? His soul would have liked to have prayed then, but his intellect was ashamed to do so, and his lips were unaccustomed. And though he had been brought up in a Christian land, he knew nothing more than a heathen about repentance from sin, and the way of Salvation through belief in the atoning blood of Jesus. Having heard it all his life he had never apprehended it. Like thousands of others it was as an idle tale, a string of words that meant nothing to him. Yet his soul was crying out for God, and he didn't know enough to take the Book, the only way of life, and find out what it all meant.

Far beyond midnight when the moon was low in the heavens he went home, and his mother waking and weeping her bitter tears, thinking her bitter thoughts, listened as he came up the stair and thought of him as having spent his evening with a girl whose fascination would fast lead him to a downward course. For such is the tried and rebuked way of those who try to walk ahead of God, and ask not for His leading. Poor, blind, self-righteous, but good intentioned Harriet Granniss!

CHAPTER VIII

THERE came days when Jud Granniss took Ariel Custer to walk in those same woods where he had thought his deep thoughts under the stars. There were Saturday afternoons, and early evenings during the longer spring twilight, and they talked of many things.

At first Ariel was shy about going anywhere with him, their acquaintance was so new, and she had been most carefully brought up; but gradually as she came to know Emily Dillon better, and then Jud himself, she yielded to his invitations.

There came a gala day when Harriet Granniss was sent as a delegate to a Missionary Conference in another part of the state, and Emily Dillon felt like a lamb let loose.

It was marvellous that Harriet had been chosen for this office for she was not exceedingly popular in her missionary society faithful as she was. But the president who usually attended these functions was taken ill with pneumonia and it became a matter of volunteering. As Harriet Granniss was the only member present at the hastily called meeting of the vice president, who said she could and would go, Harriet was sent. The vice president was a bit worried about it, for she knew the president liked to be represented by the right person who would make a good impression of their society; but she had company herself and a sick child, and it was good to get the matter settled so easily.

Harriet Granniss was pleased as a child. She bought a new dress, and a coat, and a new hat. She bought new gloves and shoes and a silk petticoat, and she went around with a ponderous importance upon her as if she were newly elected to serve as president of the United States. Emily Dillon watching said "Poor thing! She's never had much fun in her life. Perhaps that's what's the matter with her. I must try to plan to give her a good time oftener, though it's hard to know what would please her."

Harriet was to stay over two nights. She bought a new suit case and a new hand bag, and when she bade goodbye to Emily in the morning there was almost a smile upon her grim lips. She stalked away to the station carrying her own suit case refusing Emily's suggestion of a cab—Jud of course was gone to his work as she took the ten o'clock train—and she looked trim and capable and altogether an ornament to the Woman's Missionary Society of Glenside.

Emily watched her around the corner, waved a bit of a handkerchief after her, waited breathlessly till she heard the whistle of the train and the puff of its going in the distance. Then she ran in the house, shut the front door and laughed aloud!

She was still laughing as she ran upstairs, a girl's bubbling care-free laugh, though she was far past girlhood. While she made her bed and tidied her room she was singing, trilling a carol she used to know long ago before life took the singing heart out of her.

She tripped about the house putting it in order. Getting a lunch she loved, just graham pancakes and syrup, that she hadn't had since Harriet came to live with her, because Harriet said they weren't good for her. She made some cocoanut custard pudding for dinner because Jud loved it. Harriet considered cocoanut not fit to put in a human stomach. She called up the butcher—a thing Harriet never did, she said they always cheated you if you ordered that way—and ordered a porterhouse steak cut *thick*. Ordered fresh mushrooms, and new peas regardless of their price. She never even asked the price, she was so happy she didn't have to. Not that Emily was naturally a spendthrift, but that Harriet was such a savethrift that Emily felt she just must do something to celebrate this being allowed to do as she pleased. Then she went up to her room without locking the door and lay down with a book to rest awhile. Harriet would have considered that a lazy waste of time. Emily never dared read, except the newspaper a very few minutes after all work was done, without locking her door. Emily did hate to be reproved, although she had lived for the last five years in a constant state of reproof, yet she had never gotten callous to it, and always dreaded Harriet's sharp words just as much each time.

About noon when she knew that Ariel would be preparing to go out to her lunch and it wouldn't interfere with her work Emily called her office and invited her to dinner that night.

She had a wonderful time getting ready for that party. She went out to the flower shop and bought a mass of sweet peas for the table, flaming coral and white with maiden hair fern. She delved into the old highboy and brought out fine linen laid away in lavender. She opened a small silver chest where a few fine old spoons and forks were kept and spent a happy hour rubbing them bright. She climbed to the top shelf of the china closet, where Harriet had relegated her mother's best sprigged china for fear it would be broken, and joyously set the table for three with the sweet peas in a cut glass bowl in the centre. She even telephoned to the fruit store for new potatoes—Harriet considered it criminal to use them until the old ones were positively gone,—and she bought a whole pitcher of cream to use on the pudding. She even put on a little old white dimity dress she had before her father died. She hadn't worn it but once since Harriet came because Harriet said white was childish for a grown woman and besides it made so much washing.

She looked as pretty as a picture with her cheeks all rosy when Jud came home a train early and looked askance at the festive table:

"We're going to have a party, Jud?" she said with a twinkle in her eye, and when Jud tried not to frown because he liked Emily and repeated "Company!" in a disappointed way, she twinkled again and said:

"Yes. A girl."

"A girl!" he said and stepped back quickly as if he would like to go while the going was good.

Emily Dillon laughed joyously:

"It's only Ariel Custer. You won't mind her, will you Jud?"

And Jud's face wreathed all in smiles and he hastened upstairs to get ready for the guest.

They had a wonderful time that evening. They all washed the dishes together and then they played parchesi. And when they were tired of that Emily opened the old square piano and made Ariel play.

The piano was much out of tune and two keys stuck and refused to sound but it was heavenly sweet to Emily Dillon who had not opened it since her father died, and whose playing anyway was like a little bird's twittering. Her father hadn't believed in wasting good money on music lessons, and when her mother died that ended music lessons for Emily Dillon.

Ariel's fingers strayed into a hymn presently. She sang in a sweet appealing voice and Jud growled in with a tenor. Even Emily ventured a shy alto such as she sang beneath her breath in prayer-meeting when she went, and when there were enough others present to drown her voice.

It was almost twelve o'clock when Jud saw Ariel home beneath the starlight, an unheard of hour for that house when Harriet was home. But Harriet in her big mass-missionary meeting was happy and would never know how the mice were at play while she was away.

That evening did a great deal to cement the friend-ship between these three. It was that night that Ariel promised to go to church with Emily, and Jud listening decided to go to the Methodist church himself the next Sunday night.

A few weeks after her return from the Missionary Conference Harriet began to take alarm.

Jud had been careful not to walk by the house from the train with Ariel, but always managed to go around by the back street, saying he thought it was much pleas-anter and made the walk a little longer, and she laugh-ingly complied. It was pleasant to her too to walk and talk with Jud. He was her only man friend in this strange land and it was natural for her to enjoy his company.

But Harriet discovered that her son was not studying evenings as diligently as before. She noticed how often he had to go out evenings, and how frequently he stayed in town at night. And presently a minor member of the Missionary Society who lived on the block back, whose house Jud and Ariel passed at night from the train, asked Harriet while they waited for a quorum to arrive:

"Who is that pretty girl your son is going with now? I don't think she belongs in this town."

Harriet looked at her grimly and faced her down:

"My son doesn't go with any girls," she said in a tone one wouldn't like to contradict, "except now and then Helena Boggs," she added with the remembrance that where there was a will there was a way, and it was everything to create the right impression before hand.

"Oh, it wasn't Helena Boggs," said the other woman decidedly. "This one is real pretty with light hair, looks like a fairy! Oh, I know that Boggs girl. No, it wasn't her. I've seen 'em most every night coming from the train. She must live up my street somewhere."

"I think they're going to begin now," said Harriet reaching over for a hymn book, and settling back as if the matter they were talking of were of no moment. But that missionary meeting was simply destroyed so far as she was concerned. She got no enjoyment whatever out of it. She was planning what she could do to save Jud.

It was the next week that Harriet sprung a bomb on her family.

"Emily!" she said one morning when they were wiping the dishes amicably together. Matters had really been going along pretty well since Harriet's outing and Emily had been reflecting on asking her to run down to the shore a day and see how some tenement babies in whom she was interested were getting along in the baby hospital. But Emily had a sudden creepy sensation when Harriet began with that sharp high pitched "Emily!" It somehow seemed portentous.

"Yes?" said Emily with a little quick drawing of her breath that she might meet whatever was coming with her lungs full. It helped her to be more self controlled.

"I suppose I have a right to invite company when I like, haven't I? As it's half my house it's my privilege isn't it?"

"Why—certainly!" hesitated Emily with a feeling that she was somehow relinquishing blindfold her last privilege.

"Well," said Harriet wheeling to put away the tins she was wiping and clattering them sharply into their places as she talked, "I *have* anyhow! Helena Boggs is coming to stay with me while her folks go west for a few weeks. They're thinking of moving out there but Helena wants to stay here. If they decide to stay I told her there was no reason in the world why she shouldn't live here. There's that room you said I might use, and I never have. It has furniture enough, and we don't need it—"

"Oh, but, I shouldn't care to rent rooms!" said Emily anxiously. "It really isn't necessary—and—I shouldn't care for it."

"I didn't say anything about renting rooms," said masterful Harriet, "She's coming to visit me for a while. If she stays she can pay her share just as we do—"

"Would you think that was wise on your son's account?" temporized Emily.

"Wise?" snorted Harriet, "What on earth has Jud to do with that? And what business of yours is that I'd like to know?"

"Well, none of course, only I think it might be unfortunate if you drove Jud away. It might make you feel badly. I really think you would make a great mistake if you brought some one here that Jud doesn't like."

"Oh, of course you know what my son likes and doesn't like. That's just like you, Emily. But I have a little more sense than you think I have. I've made up my mind to let Jud see what other girls can be. He's determined to go with a girl that isn't fit to go with, so I'm going to give him a good wholesome chance to see a good wholesome girl right here in his own home. Those things go a whole lot by being together, and getting to know each other, and it's time he knew what the right kind of a girl was like. If he knew Helena real well he wouldn't be traipsing off nights with this scatterbrained little doll that hasn't a grain of sense in her head and isn't fit to come into a decent family."

"But where did you get such an idea as that about Ariel Custer? You're utterly mistaken, she's a lovely girl. I've seen a great deal of her lately, and I think she is one of the loveliest girls I ever knew. She comes from an old Virginia family, and has true refinement and a fine education—"

"Yes, I *thought* likely you'd been aiding and abetting Judson in this foolishness! He never would have dared start anything like this alone. He *knows me!* But you needn't think you two can put anything across over me. That girl is *not fit* for my son. How do you know she is a lovely girl, and belongs to an old family? *She* told you so, I suppose. You couldn't have found out any other way. But *I* know better. I know that a strange girl can't come into a town and set herself straight for a young man and chase after him and not give him a minute's peace, and still be a good girl. I know a nice girl doesn't come into a strange town and nobody know a thing about her. She wouldn't be a nice girl if she did. And she wouldn't live a day in that Smalley woman's house either. That's enough against her. And as if that wasn't enough, she's carried on so chasing after Jud and always walking home with him every night, going around the other street so I wouldn't see and all, that every body is talking about her. Mrs. Farley had the nerve to ask me about it last week at the Missionary Meeting and I was so embarrassed I could have fallen through the floor. To think my son should take up with a mere adventuress! And you helping it on! You're just nothing but a romantic fool, Emily Dillon! I should think you'd be ashamed! Lucky your father prevented your marrying a spineless beggar or you'd have been—"

But Harriet Granniss suddenly realized that Emily Dillon was on her way upstairs and seemed not to have heard her.

Emily went out a few minutes later and did not return all day, not until ten o'clock at night. It was quite unprecedented. Harriet eyed her suspiciously the next morning at breakfast, but she sat in her place as serene as a summer morning and said not a word about the occurrence of the morning before. Harriet had more to say and was waiting till Jud left for his train for she did not want him to know yet that the Boggs girl was coming. But when Jud got up to go Emily arose also hurriedly:

"I've a letter I wish you'd mail for me Jud," she said sweetly, "I'll get it. It's all ready."

Emily Dillon went after her letter but she did not return to the table. Harriet waited eating her toast slowly, for Emily to come back, but she stayed in her room all the morning, and by lunch time wild horses could not have dragged a word more out of Harriet Granniss' mouth. They sat grimly eating a lunch which was of purpose made scanty, and all of articles that Emily did not care for. Stewed tomatoes, fried eggs browned on both sides, and canned soup. Harriet was a good cook, but there were times that she wasn't. This was one of the times.

Emily minced at everything pleasantly, saying little and ignoring her companion's silence. She had a chastened look almost as if she had been weeping. She went back to her room as soon as the meal was over.

The Boggs girl appeared a little before six that night and there was a great sound of thumping and moving furniture in the room she had been given. Her trunk appeared just as Judson arrived from his train. He paused in the doorway with a questioning glance and waited until the expressman had gone. Then he sought the kitchen and demanded to know what had happened.

"Helena's here," said Harriet trying to act as if it were quite a common occurrence. "Her folks are gone away on a trip and she was all alone so I invited her here."

"Helena?" said Jud, puzzled.

"Yes, *Helena*," said his mother complacently, "She's a very nice girl and she's lonely. I want you to be nice to her while she's here."

"You mean that Boggs girl?" he demanded.

"I mean Helena Boggs," said Harriet evenly, "She's just as interesting as that little upstart of an A—E—Real Custard you're so smitten with. I just heard her first name yesterday and I should think that would be enough for any sensible man, A—E—real! Of all fanciful stuff and nonsense! Name a girl *that*! It's ridiculous!"

"Mother, do you mean that Boggs girl is going to be here for several days to make you a visit?"

"I do. I mean she's going to visit me until her folks come back from the West, and she'll be down to supper in five minutes so I advise you to run up and wash, and be quick about it for this potpie'll fall if we have to wait dinner."

Jud gave his mother one scathing look—which she purposely did not see because she was earnestly engaged in cutting bread,—and flung up the stairs two steps at a time.

There was sound of heavy footsteps overhead for his room was directly over the kitchen, opening of doors and bureau drawers, a stampede to the attic and down again, sound of shoes thumped on the floor, splashing of water, more heavy footsteps, and just as Harriet came into the hall to ring the little bell that summoned the house to dinner her son appeared on the stairs with a suit case in his hand and a coat slung over his arm. He pounded down stairs and out the front door:

"I'm *going*," he said to his mother as she approached with protest in her eye, "You can let me know at the office when that *horse* is gone!" and with that he vanished down the steps and out the gate.

Emily in her open doorway just above the stair landing heard it all, and glancing down saw that the Boggs girl was pausing on the stair case, two steps below, and must have heard it also. Emily retreated to her room and made pretense of hunting a sweater to let the atmosphere clear before going down, but when she reached the dining room the Boggs girl seemed serene as if nothing had happened. She and Harriet had evidently been talking it over and they seemed to have a deep laid plan. Harriet was tremendously upset by the withdrawal of her son, but the Boggs girl seemed to think it would turn out all right. They ate and laughed and talked and ignored Emily as if she had been a servant, and when she had finished a brief repast she excused herself and hurried away. She came down stairs with her hat on while the two were in the kitchen finishing the dishes and slipped out the door and up the street to find Ariel. She felt the need of moral support. Also, she hoped Jud might turn up that evening and she wanted to see him. She could not bear to have him driven out from his home. She wanted to assure him of her sympathy. She wanted to be sure that in his wrath he would not go far away nor do anything foolish.

Jud came later in the evening with a tired set look upon his face. When Emily arose presently and said she must go home he walked back to the gate with her, and told her he had taken board with a family about a mile from Glenside on the edge of another suburb, and that he did not intend to come home until the Boggs girl had left for good.

Emily did not try to persuade him. She felt only too much like following his example. She told him not to worry that she thought somehow it would all come out right, and that perhaps his staying away for a little would help his mother to understand. Also she said that she thought that the Boggs girl would be the one to show his mother just what the Boggs girl really was, and she would probably understand her mistake before long and send her away.

Jud paused beside the gate in the dark of the hedge:

"You're just awfully good, Miss Emily," he said, "I can't thank you enough. You always understand and you always do the right thing, but sometimes I'm terribly sorry for you. You needn't think I can't see how hard it's been all these years for you to have us thrust upon you this way. Of course she's my mother, and I want to take care of her and do the best I can for her, but I can't stand these girls! They get on my nerves! That Boggs girl is the limit. I don't see how you're going to stand it, Miss Emily, mother ought to see she has no right—"

"Never mind, Jud, I don't want your mother to be hampered by me, and perhaps this is the quickest way to help her to understand. But I see how it is with you, and you're not to worry. I'll take care of your mother till the time comes, if she needs it, and then I hope you'll be back with us. I shall miss you, Jud."

She put out her little rose leaf hand and Jud took it reverently. He would have liked to have kissed it but he had no precedent to teach him that it was possible. But just then his heart was very warm to this mother-touch that was not his mother, yet understood.

He gave her his address and telephone number and she promised to let him know if ever he was needed by his mother; also if she should need his help herself in any way. He told her that if things became too hard for her at any time she must let him know and he would just come home and tell that Boggs girl what he thought of her himself and put her out! But Emily Dillon told him no, it was best not. It was best to let things take their course, "and—and—Trust in God" she added shyly. It was the first time she had ever spoken of sacred things like that to him and Jud knew that she meant far more than just those simple words.

"Yes," he answered fervently, "Perhaps that will help I'm wondering if you haven't always had something big that I didn't know. I used to see you reading the Bible, Miss Emily and wondered how you could, but I'm wondering if it wasn't better—"

"Yes," said Emily timidly, "It's always better. It's the only way you can stand things sometimes. You try it Jud."

"Perhaps I will," he said huskily, and then entirely irrelevantly he suddenly said:

"Say, Miss Emily, I wish you'd go often to see A— to see Miss Custer. I feel worried about her. She doesn't say much but I don't like that man she's working for. He hasn't got a good name down town. I heard something today about him. I wish she could get away. I don't like to talk to her about it, but maybe *you* could." And Emily promised to help.

Then Jud went down the dark street to his boarding house, for he would not compromise Ariel by staying late at her house even though Mrs. Smalley had given her the use of her stuffy little parlor, in which to receive callers.

CHAPTER IX

Dick Smalley had "fallen" for Ariel, fallen hard. Her tender care and gentleness for Stubby would have done it even if she had not been so lovely herself. But Ariel was lovely as a spring morning and her frank sunny smile had won him at first sight.

They became comrades over Stubby's invalid couch,

and by the second week of the girl's stay in the house Dick was her avowed protector and admirer. He stole flowers from the station garden to present to her, he brought home magazines from the newsstand for her, he went out in the fields and gathered berries for her supper when she came home tired at night, and he hung upon her every glance with averted gaze, and would have gone to the ends of the earth at a single word from her.

She in her turn enjoyed the friendship as much as he did. She began to be interested in his lessons, to inspire him to do well in school, a thing he had always heretofore thought beneath a real boy. His teachers opened their eyes in surprise at his raised hand in class when a question was asked, He had never been eager to answer anything before. He had always sulked behind others and avoided having to recite. Now he took a real pleasure in telling in an offhand expository way what he knew. His intercourse with Ariel had given him a grown up way of looking at his lessons, and telling the answers, that the other children could not compass. They looked at him with amazement. To think that Dick had attained to talking about book knowledge like that. He gave his answers in class with an assurance that none of them ever had, no matter how well they knew their lessons. He spoke of matters of science and the geographical world with an odd manner of imparting information which he felt even the teacher didn't know. And sometimes he included an incident that Ariel had told him out of her store of knowledge gleaned from her father's library. The members of his class, even the girl who was denominated the teacher's pet, began to expect something interesting of him when he got up to recite, instead of giving him the superior smile of ridicule that had been the custom when he was called upon.

All this Ariel did for him quite unconsciously just by being interested in what he was supposed to be doing at school. He saw what importance she attached to learning and he forthwith set up learning as a thing to be followed and conquered.

She began to teach him to play on the old cabinet

organ that graced the stuffy parlor, and before many
lessons had passed he exhibited his skill on the school
piano to the intense admiration of his ring of boy followers who already worshipped him from an athletic stand
point. There was no doubt whatever but that the advent
of Ariel was the best thing that ever came into little
Dick Smalley's life. Why, he even sidled into the Methodist church sometimes with her of a Sunday evening,
and admitted he wouldn't mind going into a Sunday
School Class if she were only the teacher. The difficulty
was that Ariel's presence was so quiet and unobtrusive
that she had not been asked to take a Sunday School
class as yet. Which is a pity, for had Dick come to
Sunday School, his entire baseball team would have
joined to a man.

Dick invited Ariel to attend a baseball game one
Saturday afternoon and Jud came with her, to Dick's
overwhelming satisfaction. Jud himself was no small person in the athletic world. The boys of the High School
team often got him to coach them or to umpire a game,
and as a pitcher he was in great demand always, although at that time he had little time to give to outdoor
sports. But his presence at a game was enough to give
prestige to the team for a month or two.

Jud praised Dick's home run when he swaggered up
to them all hot and beaded with perspiration, during an
interval in the game, and they talked in terms of sports-
men. Jud treated Dick like a man and he swelled with
importance as he trudged loftily back to take his place
in the game once more his heart beating high with
happiness. He began his sentences with "Jud Granniss
says" more than once, showing his intimacy with that
great light in the baseball world, and he swayed his
team by a few well directed quotations from him, so
that they came off triumphant amid great applause from
the bleachers.

After that game Dick's adoration included Jud as well
as Ariel, and there was nothing he would not do for
them both. The world, perhaps, does not recognize what
a treasure there is in the friendship of one such boy. He
is a mine of faithfulness and chivalry, of loyalty even to

martyrdom, and of devotion unequaled. It even extended in Dick's case to a cessation on his part, of hostilities, between himself and Harriet Granniss, as soon as he discovered that Harriet Granniss was mother to his hero.

The friendship between Ariel and Jud grew with the weeks. The fact that Jud had left home made him feel strangely alone in the world, and tended to strengthen his interest in Ariel.

They did not flaunt their friendship before the world. In fact they were most quiet and circumspect about it, but Harriet Granniss lost no time in putting herself in touch with her son's every movement. There are always people enough who are willing to spy and to tell if you make it worth their while, and Harriet had a number of such emissaries among her women friends; "cats," Jud called them, but then Jud was prejudiced. He took little pains however to make the best impression before them, and perhaps Harriet Granniss was often justified in the bitter tears she shed into her pillow after the Boggs girl had left her for the night and gone to her room with a book and a fresh wad of gum. The people who kept Harriet supplied with news were not always accurate, and frequently resorted to exaggeration when facts failed to give zest to their tales. Often Emily Dillon might have told her the truth and dispelled her anxiety but Emily Dillon had no thought of all that was going on in Harriet's mind. She went her serene quiet way, and tried to feel as little as possible the obnoxious presence of Helena Boggs who seemed to have become a fixture in the house. Life had not led her to expect a pleasant pathway.

Harriet Granniss was going on her grim determined way with the Boggs girl despite the defection of Jud. By sheer force of will she seemed to think she could bring him back again to submit to her plans for his life. Jud came home once or twice for some of his belongings, and held brief fiery talks with his mother. He never came without first telephoning Emily Dillon to find out if the Boggs girl was away from the house. The last time he came he packed his trunk and cleaned the room of every scrap that belonged to him. What he did not want to keep he carried down and burned in the back yard. Then he called his mother from her room where she had remained silently during his labors and delivered an ultimatum. He was not coming back again *ever* unless she sent that girl away!

Harriet made a thin hard line of her colorless lips and said she would *never* send the Boggs girl away: that he was an unnatural son, and that he had no right to demand anything while he was going with a girl who was so obnoxious to his mother. She began to state that Ariel must be some relation to the "offscouring of the earth" whatever that may be, but Jud refused to discuss Ariel with his mother. He said she had shown herself too utterly unfair to be worthy to judge; that he was not worthy to unfasten Ariel's shoes, but he meant to marry her some day if she would have him, so she might as well get used to the idea at once; and that if she had any idea of being a mother at all she would stop such outrageous talk about a lovely and innocent girl and go and see her and do the right thing. He knew it would be a long time before he would have money enough to marry a girl like Ariel who had been used to everything that money could buy, and nothing was too good for, but he never should change, and he would never return if the Boggs girl did not go, nor so long as his mother talked that way about the girl he loved.

Then with a sudden impulse his face softened and he went and stood before his mother:

"Mother," he pleaded, just as he used to do on rare occasions sometimes when he was a little boy and wanted something very much, "Mother, why will you be this way? Why won't you listen to reason and go and see Ariel, and be a mother to us both? You have power to make me very happy—"

"Happy, Oh, yes! *You* would be happy! But what about *me?*" screamed Harriet Granniss hardly, "You want to walk right over my heart! Marry a huzzy that never could be my daughter! Well, take what you've brought

on yourself and me then! Work your fingers to the bone
if you will. She'll be faded and old by the time you can
ask her to marry you—a light complected girl like that,—
or else she'll get tired waiting for you and marry the
rich man she works for. If you marry a girl I like I can
fix it so you can set up housekeeping right away. There's
money your father left, enough to start you, that you
weren't to have until you were thirty unless I approved
the woman you married. I'll never approve that yellow
haired baby-doll. Understand that, Judson Granniss! But
if you'll marry Helena I'll see that you get it right away.
It's enough to set you up in business!"

Jud faced his mother, white with anger:

"I'd see myself dead first," he said furiously. "Marry
that great *slob!* Mother you're enough to make a man
lose his soul!"

And Harriett Granniss' son turned and left her.

She stood a long time in his empty room looking out
across the fields that skirted the back yard, her lips set
thin and hard, a terrible expression in her determined
eyes. The iron had entered her soul! She had lost her
son, she knew, out of her life forever. He might forgive in
a way but he never would feel the same toward her
again. The dream she had dreamed of his life and hers
flowing in a long pleasant stream as she had planned it,
would never come true now. But she would not give up!
Something hardened within her, sour and bitter and
painful. If one can age in a moment Harriet Granniss
could have been said to age in that hour when she and
her son parted in the dismantled room, and he went
away to work for the girl she hated because he hated
the girl she had picked out for him.

They walked in the woods together that evening,
Ariel and Jud because it was the only place where they
could really talk without fear of interruption. Each had
seen a cloud in the other's eyes, and each longed to
comfort the other. But Jud tried to shake off his de-
pression when he saw the trouble in the girl's eyes:

"Has anything gone wrong, Ariel?" he asked. They had

reached the stage of calling each other familiarly by the first name.

"Oh, I guess not," said the girl wearily, "I sometimes think I'm hard to please."

"What is it?—" he almost added "dear" but caught it just in time, "Is it that man? Is he hard on you? I'd like to wring his neck for him!"

She laughed but her voice sounded like a sob:

"I guess I'm just tired," she said, "I can't quite get used to ways up North."

"What ways?"

"Why, such familiar ways. I'm afraid I made Mr. Martin angry—but—Well, I'm not used to such things."

"Did he try to be familiar with you?" Jud bristled thunderously.

"Why, I don't think he called it that. He seemed to think it was nothing at all. He keeps putting his hand on mine, wanting to shake hands in the morning, and makes it such a prolonged ceremony that I finally mustered courage to ask him please not, that I wanted to respect him and myself too; and he didn't like it. He said I had insinuated something that he never meant—He, well he made me feel that *I* was the guilty one, not he. I never was so mortified and confused in my life. I couldn't do a thing all the afternoon and he went around looking hurt and offended. I know I made a thousand mistakes in today's letters, and I'll probably be dismissed. I don't know what I'll do if I am, because I've been spending my small capital while I was waiting for my raise, and I just got it last week you know."

Jud's face was stern and hard:

"The beast!" he said under his breath, and clenched his nails hard into the palms of his hands, "And yet you say a God knows and cares for you!"

"Oh, don't Jud!" said Ariel with quick realization of where her complaint was leading her, "You mustn't think that! I do say God is caring, and I know somehow it will come out all right. I'm glad you reminded me. It wasn't right for me to get downhearted. I guess I've not been praying as much as I ought lately. Oh, Jud! Don't look like that! Don't think such things! And I've been praying so hard that you too might trust him. Is seems sometimes that I can't stand it not to have my one friend know Him, my Heavenly Father!"

Jud's face softened:

"Well, how can I help it, little girl? I can't bear to see you in a rotten hole like that and think a God who loves you lets things like that happen to you. I'm in a rotten hole myself. If your God would help us out of this and put us in a plain simple path where things were decent— I wouldn't ask much—why perhaps I would trust Him. I'd like to, for your sake, because you want it, and because it seems to give you so much comfort. God knows I need comfort myself. But how can I trust Him when things are all wrong this way? How can I believe He cares? What did He make us for if it was only to suffer?"

"Well, I don't know that I can answer all those questions," said Ariel earnestly, "but I know that you can't make conditions with God. You've got to trust Him through hard things before you get the assurance of His love. Oh, Jud, I wish you'd just take Him right now and trust Him for all you're worth? Won't you?"

They were sitting on a great rock by the edge of a little stream that wandered down from the wooded hillside. Across the fields a young moon was rising and the sky was luminous with the fading of the just departed sunset. She lifted the blue of her eyes to his earnest anxious glance and their young troubled lives seemed to stop and stand still in sudden revelation of one another:

Suddenly, out of the silence Jud spoke:

"I *will*, Ariel. If you say that's right, and you want me to, I will, so far as I know how, trust Him. I'll try it and see what comes."

"Do you mean you will stick by Him whatever comes?"

"Do you mean I'm to stick even if I can't believe?"

"I mean you're to *believe* even if you can't *understand*," said Ariel earnestly.

He gave her another long look.

"Well, then," he said at length, solemnly "so far as in me lies, *I will!*"

Their hands had stolen together in a solemn clasp and neither of them seemed to notice it. There was nothing in it of the familiarity to which Ariel had been objecting earlier in the evening, and yet it was the sweetest possible familiarity.

"Then," said Ariel after a moment of silent joy, "I'm *glad!* That's the greatest thing that could come! If you'll keep that vow nothing else can really hurt."

"Do you care so much?"

"Yes, I care—so much!" said the girl with a deep ring to her voice. "It's the only thing in the world you know that *really* matters *forever.*"

His hand held hers closely, reverently. He was very still watching her face in the twilight. Wondering at the great joy within him. Wondering just what effect this vow he had made was to have on his whole life. Wondering if it really meant all that it seemed now that he had made it?

Ariel's voice broke the silence softly:

"Won't you tell me what was troubling you?"

He was still again for sometime:

"I oughtn't to—" he said wearily, "but I want to," he added, as if he could not resist the temptation.

"Why oughtn't you to?" she asked gently.

"Because it might make you feel—badly! It might spoil—our friendship."

"Well," said Ariel, "I'd rather feel badly if I can sympathize with you or help any. And as for our friendship, I don't feel anything can spoil that. There are things that might put us apart, of course, but that couldn't spoil a friendship that is founded on God."

"You are wonderful!" said Jud reverently.

"Then you will tell me what is troubling you?"

"Yes, I will tell you. It is that I love you, and I want to take care of you, to take you away from that beast of a man you are working for, and put you where no one can trouble you any more; and I don't see any way to do it, not yet."

"Oh," said Ariel startled, her cheeks growing warm in

the darkness, and her hands suddenly becoming conscious of their enfolding, "Oh, but that is—very wonderful—I did not think—I did not know it would be anything like that—!"

CHAPTER X

IT WAS about a week after their walk upon the hillside that Jud came upon the bungalow.

The train had been unusually long and crowded that night and stopped far down the track so that when Jud got off he found himself a block nearer his boarding place if he went across the fields and took a side street where a new building operation was in progress, than if he went up to the station as usual. The little stone bungalow was all finished, and attracted him at once. With all his hurry he had to stop and glance in. The sight filled him with a great longing and he took Ariel to see it that night.

It was a little wonder in the way of a small home. To begin with there were two large hemlock trees in one corner of the lot that gave it a look of having been there sometime, and being able to stay and give comfort, a sort of finished, homey look.

The living room was big and roomy with a fireplace of stone and soft creamy walls of rough plaster. It had windows on three sides, the front one a great glazed arch, and built-in seats and bookcases that made it seem almost furnished already. The dining room and kitchen had window charms of their own with many little tricks of convenience hidden away in unexpected spaces and crannies, china closets and ironing board, and tiny refrigerator room. And there were two bed rooms and a bath. Outside the wide tiled terrace was partly covered by an overhang supported by stone arches. It seemed a dream dropped down from heaven to those two poor young wayfarers, and they stood with close clasped hands and gazed at it awhile before they even dared to venture in.

They knew it for their heart's desire even before they had gone together from room to room discovering its charms and delights, hunting out its secret contrivances for comfort and convenience. And then, as evening dropped down and the shadows crept within the empty rooms, and found them standing in front of the great stone fireplace, Ariel turned with a sound almost like a sob and dropped her face against Jud's rough coat sleeve:

"Oh, Jud, doesn't it seem just like heaven?" she said, and within Jud's heart was born the great unconquerable desire to get it for her.

They sat down in the darkened room on the seat by the fireplace and talked it over—all their slender resources.

"I have some furniture," said Ariel, "a lovely old table and chest, and some chairs. There's a great big mahogany bed that was my mother's, and two chests of drawers, some mirrors, and a big old clock. They're down in Virginia, but it would cost a lot to get them up here."

"We could manage that," said Jud thoughtfully, "if we only had the house to put them in. I know a fellow with a truck. We might manage to go down after them. Perhaps we could take that on our wedding trip."

"Oh," said Ariel—"But do you suppose Mr. Martin would let me off for a wedding trip?"

"Mr. Martin be hanged!" said Jud fiercely, "Do you suppose I'm going to let my wife work for any Mr. Martin? Ariel, I just must get another job. I'm sure there are jobs somewhere that pay better than mine. Perhaps there is some one somewhere that would buy this house and rent it to us, let us pay a big rent and let it go on buying it. Perhaps I could borrow!— Say, Ariel, that's an idea! There is such a thing as a Building Association. We ought to be able to buy a house without paying much down."

"But we haven't anything to pay down," laughed

Ariel, almost on the verge of tears she wanted the dear little house so much.

"There must be a way," said Jud, "There must! I wonder—if only my mother could be made to see things right—!"

But he wouldn't say any more about his thought that night. He suggested that they go out and walk, and Ariel wise in her generation complied.

As they walked away from the street she looked back and said:

"See, Jud, doesn't it look sweet in the moonlight! If we can't have that one maybe we'll have one like it some day. Let's begin to save right away. I've thought of something I can do without—already!"

"There's to be no doing without for you, Ariel, you've had enough of that already."

"Oh, but it wouldn't be doing without. It would be doing for the house instead of something else."

"You wait, Ariel. I've got an idea!" said Jud, "But first, we've got to find out the price of the house. It may be way up in the clouds. Those unusual things usually are you know."

"Yes, I know," sighed Ariel, "But maybe we can get something big to do. I'm sure if I lived in a house like that I could work twice as hard."

"You're not going to work when I get the say so," growled Jud joyously.

Ariel's laugh rang out at that:

"What would you have, Jud, a sluggard for a wife?"

> "*Lazy* Bird, *Lazy* Bird
>   Wilt thou be mine,
> Thou shalt not wash dishes
>   Nor yet feed swine,
> But sit on a cushion and
>   Sew a fine seam
> And feed upon strawberries,
>   Sugar and cream,"

chanted Ariel mockingly

"Well, you may have to wash a few dishes for a little

while till I get the house paid for, but you jolly well won't write letters for that old swine of a Martin, when I get you, understand that!"

Ariel sighed:

"Then we will have to wait for years and years," she complained sweetly, "if you don't let me help buy the house."

They spent an hour and a half arguing the matter, and finally compromised on finding her another position with a woman writer somewhere who was to be providentially provided for their need; and they parted for the night and went happily to their rest to dream of the little stone bungalow.

A week later there was a National holiday, and as Mr. Martin was away on a business trip not even he could require Ariel's presence in the office all day, so they planned for a long talked of holiday.

The night before Jud came down to Smalley's for a few minutes to tell her he had seen the owner of the bungalow at last. He had been away in Chicago and just got back the night before.

The bungalow proved to be remarkably low, and two thousand was all that was required down.

"Two thousand dollars!" said Ariel aghast, "Why it might as well be two million as far as we are concerned!" Her whole slender figure drooped pitifully. Dreams of the pretty little home vanished. Then suddenly she sat up brightly:

"Never mind, Jud. We musn't be grumpy. There are other houses in the world, and you can't tell what good thing our Father has in store for us. Remember, our lives are His planning, not our own. It doesn't seem as if there could be anything else better than this little house in the whole wide world, but there must be, and we'll trust and not be afraid, won't we?"

Jud's arm stole about her adoringly:

"It's easier to trust for myself than for you," he said tenderly, "but I'm doing my best at both. But listen, dear, I've just a little glimmer of hope that all isn't hopeless yet—"

She caught her breath and waited:

"You know I told you I had some money that would be mine in four years—"

"Yes?"

"It's five thousand dollars."

"But how will that help any now, Jud? Do you mean we'll have to wait four years?"

"I've been hoping I might be able to borrow on the strength of it. I don't know whether it can be done, or whether maybe mother will prevent it if she has to know, but I think it's worth trying out. There's an old friend of my father's living at Mercer, old Judge Bonner. He would know if anybody would all about my father's will and what hope there is if any of my being able to get hold of the money any sooner. It may be that he would be able to persuade mother. I haven't seen him since I was a boy and I don't know just how things stand. I never bothered about it before—"

Jud had not told Ariel of his mother's bitterness against her. He had vaguely stated that she had a girl she wanted him to go with and it had created an estrangement between them for the time being; but he had not told her that the opposition extended to herself more than in general, neither did she know all the details of the strange will. In fact she had thought little about the matter save to regret that Jud's mother was making him trouble, for she was so happy in her comradeship with him that she needed no one else to make her happiness complete. She had not questioned Jud; and it was also true that Jud had been so engrossed with the wonder of her love that he had not given much care to anything else. It was not from intention that he was keeping the ugly side of his life from her knowledge, although his natural wish would of course have been to protect his mother from being judged any more harshly than was necessary. After all she was his mother, and perhaps she would yet see the light; though he felt sure that nothing short of a miracle would bring her to that. Jud was also sensitive that his own mother should show no more motherly love toward him. He could not bear to have the girl he loved know how hard she had been to him; how she had used her power with his sick father at the last, to put him, her son, in her power until he was beyond the likelihood of marrying to displease her. It all seemed so sordid and ugly, so far from the things this girl would expect of a mother. He had been hoping against hope that something would turn up that would make it unnecessary for Ariel to know the worst. If his mother could only see her, know her in circumstances that would make her see. He even yet after all these years had hope that there was that in her mother heart that would be reached by the right appeal. He could not get away from that gentle voice of his father saying: "She's all the mother you've got, Jud, all the mother you've got."

So they laid their heavenly sweet plans and watched the clouds every night and morning to see what the weather would be, and arranged to go anyway rain or shine, because they could at least go to Mercer together even if it poured, and Ariel could wait in the post office or grocery store while Jud went on his errand to Judge Bonner. Of course, if it were pleasant they would have their wonderful day together, and it was to be down by the old Copple's Creek, where Jud used to play as a boy. He was going to show her the old swimming hole, and the rocks, and the rapids, and the place where the yellow asters grew thick like a blaze of sun, and the strip of chestnut woods where he gathered chestnuts, and the turn of the stream where the willow stood and the bull frogs sang "Ca-Chug!" right under the canoe, and the green quiet shade where the hemlocks dipped and lifted their feathery boughs in lacy canopy over mossy banks broidered out with little red berry vines and bits of baby cones.

All this and more Jud told her of the spot he used to love as a boy, and the night before she could hardly sleep thinking of the day she was to have. Not since the old dear days down in Virginia with her father and mother and grandmother had she been so happy anticipating an outing. Her happy soul lay wakeful in her hard little bed and looked into the day that was before her.

And Jud, he too lay waking, planning what he would

say and just how he would approach the question of the will and his money with the old Judge. For the joy of his outing depended on how well he succeeded first in his mission.

CHAPTER XI

ARIEL CUSTER and Judson Granniss left the trolley at Copple's Crossing and walked down the country road silently. Jud carried a square box neatly wrapped, tied and fitted with a wooden handle, and Ariel swung a grape-basket nervously. There was about them in spite of their gravity a little air of suppressed excitement, as if there were a holiday somewhere lurking about under difficulties.

At the foot of Copple's Hill they paused and Ariel took the box, Jud searching the high ground above him for a familiar landmark.

"There it is, Ariel that old hemlock with the big rock in front of it. That's a good place to wait. You can see the whole town, and not be seen by people passing in the road. I hope you won't have long to wait, for whatever comes we're going to have the day at the old creek. Don't get lonesome or worried. You know I may have to wait awhile myself, but I won't be a minute longer than I can help."

"Don't you worry about me, Jud. Stay all day if it's necessary. I've got the lunch, you know."

She wrinkled her delicate, wistful face into a wan smile.

He gave her a grave smile in return, and lifting his cap, strode away down the road. She watched him a moment with a look like a prayer, and then sped lightly up the path.

Everything about Ariel suggested her name in spite of the brooding anxiety that looked out from her eyes. She was such a frail wisp of a girl, so delicately featured, her hair so soft and wavy about her face catching the sunshine with such unexpected red and gold lights. There were lurking dimples near the droop of her lips, and hidden glints in the green-gray eyes when they were not clouded with trouble. The little faded but bravely starched green organdie she wore had a courageous grace all its own that gave her going an airy flight. She seemed to blow up to the old hemlock and the big gray rock like a pale-green moth, and drift into the hillside as if she belonged. She settled down on the cushion of moss, took off the home-made organdie hat, and rested her head back against the tree-trunk. The sunshine sifting down lacily through the pattern of the pines laid a sudden shower of gold on the halo of her hair and glorified her, all quietly, like a thing God loves.

Below her was the dusty summer road, Judson Granniss walking steadily, grimly on, and the little village in the cup of the valley not far away. She could see the church-spire, a white one with a bell, on a shady street of white houses with green blinds and brick sidewalks. The "Judge" might live in any one of those white houses, or he might have a dusty office in the little group of business buildings that clustered farther on. Ariel wished she were a bird, that she might fly over Mercer and watch where Jud went. It seemed somehow as if she might be able to discern more easily the outcome of his errand if she could but know what kind of house the man he sought lived in. He would be an old man, for he had been older than Judson's father, and had been his friend as well as lawyer. Would he be kindly and helpful, or would he be hurried and careless and hard? So many people in Ariel's life had been hard.

Two men in a Ford came clattering by. One looked up and pointed.

"Ain't that a woman settin' up there? Queer time o' day fer a woman to be loafin' round like that, Si," he commented. "Oughtta be home tendin' to her house, I should say! Young, too. Look at her hair!"

But Ariel's eyes were down the road, watching the steadily receding figure of the young man, and the wind was the other way, so that she could not hear.

The sun mounted high and the crickets down in the grass at the edge of the road sent out a rusty hum. Cicadas in the trees shot forth their sizzling voices over the sun-beaten road. The shimmer of heat hovered over the little shut-in village in the valley, and the red barns on the outskirts sat sullen and hot in the yellow sunshine. But up where Ariel sat with her throbbing, eager heart and her anxious eyes that steadily watched the white dusty ribbon of a road, there was a cool breeze and a lacy canopy of shade from the heat, and back in her mind was the sweet coolness of the creek to which they were going for the day when Jud came back. Whatever Judge Bonner said, they were going to have the day.

The sun grew hotter and stole under her shelter, laying burning, riotous fingers on her bright hair and forehead till she had to move further back in deeper shade. A bell sounded out from the white steeple, tolling, a solemn knell. She could see people coming, like black puppets in the distance, walking slowly in time with the bell, and a line of cars and carriages straggled presently across the Main Street. A faint premonition filled her soul. It was a funeral, going to the church. She could see the open door, the groups of slowly filing neighbors, and the little pageant of the village life unrolled before her. She wondered idly who was dead and what it meant to the village, what it meant to some one near and dear? Did it mean as much as Judson's errand to Judge Bonner meant to her and Jud? Then suddenly a constriction seized her throat, and her small hands worked nervously. What if it should be Judge Bonner! What if they were too late!

It seemed a long time the bell tolled, and then the people came out bearing a flower-laden coffin, and the procession crept down the street, the bell still tolling, and wound its way out across the valley and up among the hills out of sight. It must have been the realization that the bell had ceased at last to echo that dull thud within her soul that brought her eyes back again to the road and Judson Granniss returning. She knew with her first glimpse that he had no good news, else he would have been looking up and waving at the first sight of her. He walked with a plodding, dogged slump which he had adopted of late, a kind of hopeless sag of his whole fine being, and her own strong spirit rose with the need and soared like the Ariel that she was. What if he *had* tried and failed? There would be something else to do. There was always something else to do. They would go into the coolness of the woods and think of something else. Surely, not for a paltry two thousand dollars would all their sweet hopes be allowed to fade. She would tell him so at once. She would let him know he was not to despair.

She rose from her mossy seat and waved the little organdie hat, but he did not look up nor see her until he had climbed the hill and stood just before her, and there was something inexpressibly sorrowful in his face, so that she could not voice the words she had ready with which to cheer him.

"He is dead!" he said, tonelessly.

"Dead! Oh!" There was shocked grayness in her eyes. The jade lights were gone. "Then that was his funeral!"

"Yes. I had to go to it."

"Somehow I guess I knew it."

She whispered the words sadly.

"If I had only gone last week when you first suggested it!"

The eternal mother sprang up in her face. The jade lights flickered out. The girl lifted her delicate face vitally as if by main force her unconquerable spirit would pull his unconquerable spirit back to the high road of courage

"It is all right," she said, lightly. "If there had been any help for us there God would not have let him die yet. And besides, we are no worse off than before we thought of it."

His face showed utter dejection. He did not answer

A truck-load of hardware lumbered noisily down the

road below, and a stentorian voice bellowed raucously:

"The mahogany is dusty!
All the pipes are very rusty!"

The sound struck lacerating across the raw nerves of the two. Ariel shuddered.

"Let's get away from here!" She caught his hand and drew him. "Come! This is our day, whatever happens. you said so! Smile, Jud, and come find that creek for me you talk so much about."

She danced lightly on ahead as he lifted pained eyes and tried to smile. Her eyes were all jade now and very clear. She was the spirit of Ariel weaving a spell. In spite of him his spirits rose.

"This way," he said, and parted the underbrush, letting her into a cool, deep path that led across the ridge and down over rocks and pines and little green vines among mossy places with a glimpse of water far below. But he was silent as he went, and presently she stopped in front of him.

"Now," she said, gravely, "Let's sit down here and have it out. Then let's put it away forever. Tell me all about it. You'll have to, and then forget it. How did you find out?"

"I went to his house first, I remembered the way well when I got on the street. The fifth white house up the street, with the Colonial pillars. I remember father taking me with him when he put the mortgage on the house the time he was sick and couldn't work any more, after Jake Dillon had done him out of the money he loaned him.

"I was all the way up the front walk before I noticed the crepe on the door and the people inside. They thought I had come to the funeral, I suppose. I asked for the Judge, and they said 'Yes, just step in,' and before I knew what was happening I stood beside his coffin looking down into his dead face. It was awful!"

The girl's hand stole comfortingly up and down the man's coat-sleeve, and a tender, pitiful look came into her eyes, now all gray lights.

"They were just beginning the service. I had to wait, of course. Afterward, when they were taking him to the church I asked a few questions and found that a man by the name of Gouger had been looking after his affairs at the office during a long illness. They took me over to the church and coming out I met Gouger, but he said he was a newcomer and never knew anything about the Judge's old business. He said my father's will was too long ago for him to know about. The Judge was the only man who could have helped anyway. He always had a good deal of influence with mother. I was counting on him to make her see sense. She knows she has no right to keep me out of my measley little five thousand dollars just because she doesn't choose to like you." He had forgotten that he had never fully explained the thing to Ariel, but the girl somehow seemed to understand.

"It isn't as if she were getting the benefit of the money, either. It's just lying there in the bank waiting till I'm thirty years old, unless she likes the girl I pick out. She had no right to get set against you. It isn't you anyway, you know. It's just because she likes that Boggs girl and wants me to marry her. She's hardly laid eyes on you."

His brow drew together in a heavy frown, and his hand stole out and gathered Ariel's delicate one into a tender grasp.

Ariel breathed a little sigh and rested her head against his shoulder.

"Jud, it was kind of queer for your father to make it that way wasn't it? Seems as if it wasn't quite right. You had a right to your own choice, and when a man gets married is when he needs a little money if it's ever going to do him any good."

"Well, my father always was the gentle kind, and mother got her way. I can remember when I was a kid. Of course I was still young when he died and she probably worked on his feelings. But mother was always kind of jealous and wanted to run things. It's her way. She likes money, and she likes power. She likes to know she has power over me."

The gray eyes lifted bravely.

"Well, what's the difference? You can make your way.

I'm not afraid!" and the delicate hand fluttered up and down his sleeve soothingly.

"That's not getting the little stone bungalow, Ariel, and two thousand down was dirt-cheap for it. I could have worked off the mortgage in ten years even with any sort of chance. I didn't tell you, but I had made up my mind to ask the Judge to buy that property and let me rent or buy it from him."

"There'll be other bungalows," said Ariel, with a sacrificial look in her eyes; "and besides, if we can't we can't. We've just got to be content."

"I can't be content with you in the office with a man like that! He's hard as nails. I don't trust him. Sometimes he looks to me like a monster only waiting his time to devour you, and I can imagine him crunching you with delight and smacking his lips. I can't get away from the thought. No, you needn't say I'm jealous. Jealousy implies a lack of trust in you, and I haven't that, you know. It's the man. You don't know men, Ariel."

The girl did not speak at once but she looked as if she knew more than she was willing to tell. There was about her expression a kind of withdrawing, a set look to her lips, an unpleasantly reminiscent pain in her eyes. She averted her face.

"I think—I can take care of myself," she said at last, with a kind of gentle dignity that seemed to know whereof it spoke.

"Well, but I don't want you to have to take care of yourself that way, dear. If it weren't for feeling you are all alone in the world, I'd take that chance to go to the Philippines for two years, and come back rich—that is rich for us. Just think of it, two hundred and fifty a month, and absolutely no expense whatever. I could save it all, and in two years—"

"Two years would pass, I suppose, but Jud—it would be an awful while—and—would it pay, even for the money? There must be some other way. When do you have to answer him?"

"Next week."

"Lots of things might happen before that," said Ariel, brightly. "Let's forget it now and be happy just today!"

He sprang to his feet and lifted her with an answering smile. He felt comforted in spite of himself, and together they wandered down the pine-strewn path to the border of the creek.

A wonderful day they had of it, threading the winding paths through the woods, scaling great lichen-covered rocks, swinging down the border of the creek where dark hemlocks leaned their feathery branches, and wild strawberry-vines broidered the moss; eating their lunch on a flat rock in a clearing above the bank where a chorus of birds kept high carnival for their benefit; resting on the pine-needles, with the high, clear notes of the thrushes far overhead. The drowsy hum of the crickets, the chirp of an occasional tree-toad, the stillness and the beauty, all made it a perfect day, and they combined to keep their trouble in the background.

It was toward the end of the wonderful afternoon. They had found an old canoe drawn up by a rude landing, and Granniss had sought its farmer owner and paid for the privilege of its use for an hour. And they drifted up the cool, winding water way the young man paddling silently, and watching the distance with eyes that were persistently seeking a solution for his problem, the girl roused to bring him back to the day, and the beauty, and help him forget.

"I'd like to bring Miss Emily Dillon here sometime," she said, grasping the first idle thought that passed in her mind, "I think she would enjoy it."

Granniss' eyes came back to her face with a smile.

"That's a pleasant thought; we will. She doesn't have much fun in her life, though goodness knows why. She has money enough and no one to hinder her doing as she pleases, unless perhaps mother is a kind of brake on her pleasant propensities. Mother has a way of doing that to those around her; not that she intends to, but she seems to somehow compel the people in her vicinity to walk as she walks and think as she thinks. I've often thought how hard it must be for Miss Emily to have to live with mother, and why they had to be wished on each other for the rest of their natural lives. But Miss Emily is a patient little old sport, and you'd never guess it from her manner. She's just as sweet to mother and me as if she'd invited us there instead of having us put into the house that ought to be her own."

"But I don't understand," said Ariel, opening her eyes wide. "Isn't the house Miss Emily's?"

"It is and it isn't," laughed Granniss. "You see, old Jake Dillon was an old reprobate, drank and gambled and got all his relatives down on him hard so that the cousins on both sides wouldn't speak to him on the street. Then he finished matters up by dying and leaving a great deal more property than anyone dreamed he had, but he didn't leave a cent to any of his relatives except his daughter, and he tied that up pretty well too. But he left part of the house to my mother, on condition that she make it her home and make a home for his daughter, so that she need never be left alone. It was mighty hard on Miss Emily, for her ways and mother's are as unlike as winter and summer. I think it was old Jake's idea of justice, evening things up for mother after the way he'd made father lose all his money. He knew mother hadn't enough to keep her, and I suppose his conscience troubled him; so he gave mother a home for life and money enough to keep her comfortably. If Miss Emily dies first the house goes entirely to mother. It was a rank way to treat his daughter, for she had never laid eyes on mother till the day of the funeral; but she took it sweetly and patiently, and she won't go back on her father, even though all the cousins have done their level best to get her to break the will. She's polite to her cousins when they come to see her, but she never visits them, and I've often thought she was a mighty lonely little person."

"When we get a home of our own we'll invite her over a lot," said Ariel, with a sweet glow in her eyes.

"That we will!" said Granniss. "We'll show her a good time as often as we can."

"I told her about the bungalow," said Ariel. "She seemed very glad."

"She would," said Granniss, thoughtfully. "She's that way. She's unselfish. And she certainly is a good sport and enjoys things. Once when I was a kid she took me to an International Base Ball game! She pretended she wanted to see it herself. It was great! The way she sat up with her eyes sparkling! Mother never did find that out! Poor mother! She wouldn't have understood. She thought I oughtn't to *want* to go, and she would have blasted Miss Emily forever as a hopeless idiot. But I believe in my soul Miss Emily enjoyed that game as much as I did. She was just like a young girl that day, sat up laughing with her eyes shining, and clapping at the crisis of the game. She used to give me books and candy, too. That's one reason why I hated to go away from the house altogether when mother insisted on having that Boggs girl there so much. Miss Emily used to like to have me run into her sitting-room with the evening papers and talk to her a few minutes at night, and I know now she's lonesome without anybody."

"I'll run over and see her awhile tonight if we get home in time," said Ariel. "I'd have gone before if I'd realized. She's asked me, but I always hated to go on account of meeting your mother. I thought it might make things worse."

"I wish you would," said Granniss. "She would love to have you, I know. And now, I guess we better be turning back if we don't want to get caught in the woods in the dark. There's no moon tonight, and I mustn't let you get too tired if you've got to go back to work tomorrow."

CHAPTER XII

THAT same afternoon Emily Dillon had opened her bedroom-door cautiously and looked out into the hall, listened for a second and then tiptoed to the front window. Yes, it was as she had thought, Harriet Granniss was going out. Motionless in the shadow of the window-curtain she watched Harriet Granniss go down the front walk, between the flaring rows of portulacas that Harriet had planted without asking Emily if she liked them, to the ornate front gate painted white and swung between two ostentatious white pillars at the opening of the modest hedge, that Harriet had caused to be erected also without consulting her housemate in the matter. One could see at a single glance of Emily Dillon's refined cameo face that she never would have been the kind of woman to select portulacas for a border to the front walk, nor perpetrate an elaborate portal in the midst of the green simplicity of the old hedge.

That she allowed both to be, grew out of the quiet strength of her fortified life. Anyone seeing Emily Dillon seated in the dim end of the old Dillon pew under the gallery of the Methodist church, her eyes closed and her gentle head bent in prayer, would never have guessed that under the simple dark-blue-taffeta blouse there often raged a tempest of rebellion and that portulacas and front gateways and many other things of like kind were causes for many prayers that went up from a much tried heart.

Harriet Granniss, sitting heavily and importantly in the middle aisle seat of the new Congregational church would have been most astonished could she have known that her beautiful borders, and her noble front-gate architecture were the reason of so many prayers for patience. It seemed to her she had been a benefactor and she nursed a continual grievance that her efforts were not appreciated.

It was not often that Emily Dillon took the trouble to demur at any of Harriet Granniss' suggestions, because it was always long before she heard the last of it; for Harriet Granniss knew how to maintain a hunger strike better than the best suffragette that was ever arrested, and she could go around a house with a hurt look and a sigh or two, and break the spirit of any human that dared to speak and call its soul its own against her. A few intensive treatments of this sort had finished any opposition Emily Dillon might have offered with regard to trivial details concerning her home and the way it should be ordered. She simply decided that it was not worth while to have trouble. About the matter of re-painting the house pea-green with white trimming and an old-rose roof, she did hold her ground, maintaining that gray and white were the colors her father had always chosen, and gray and white was what it must be, until in haughty wrath Harriet Granniss gave in for gray, and ordered the paint. But such a gray! The kind that makes you think of blue and pink not quite well-mixed in the body, and fairly shouting in its deep contrast to the white trimmings. Emily Dillon looked at the com-pleted work aghast when she viewed it for the first time on her return from a trip up in the country where she had gone to attend the funeral of an old school-friend, and help the family get settled into life again. After that she seldom ventured to demur at anything Harriet Gran-niss suggested. She felt sure if she did that Harriet would make it turn out worse in the end. It was better to keep still and bear it.

Harriet Granniss walked firmly and heavily on her heavy feet that were shod with pointed, tapering shoes that bulged over the too-small soles. She settled down into the walk with every step she took as if she liked to leave an impression. Her large-figured voile dress swung massively about her ample form and a round lace collar lay flatly around her shoulders and chest below a cush-iony neck. Her features were heavy, and her chin and jaw were firm and set. She always wore a here-am-I air, and people seldom failed to notice it. Her hair had a natural wet crinkle under her rampant black toque, and her face was flushed with heat, but there was a bloom of talcum dusted over it, and lying in little-moist drifts in the creases of her neck. She was neatness itself and well groomed, and she knew it. She was proud of the big old cameo that fastened her collar, and she unfurled her dark-blue sun-umbrella like a banner and set forth to a missionary porch-meeting. She walked as one who has conquered all behind her and is sweeping on to triumphs new. She loved such functions, especially the tea and little cakes that were always served. She often told Emily that it was a shame *she* didn't take more interest in her church and its organizations. It wasn't right for a woman to stick at home as she did. But Emily only smiled.

Emily watched the portly figure of her housemate swing down the quiet street, a dominant person with the stiff little feathers on her smart new toque standing erect and defiant against the summer breeze. Emily's expression was meek, almost sad, rather detached, without bitterness. There was a pink pucker about her pleasant lips as of one who has borne oppression long but without the usual resultant bitterness. A little tremulous smile was always hovering in the offing ready to slip out when no one was about.

When Harriet had passed out of sight Emily turned with a quick, birdlike motion and hurried down the back stairs to the kitchen, a light of interest in her gentle blue eyes like one who climbs for a stolen pot of jam.

"You almost done, Becky?" she asked of the sad-faced, dreary-eyed woman who was ironing a blue-checked apron by the window.

"Yep! Just about. Only got two three more pieces," and she stooped to the basket underneath her board and shook out a towel, a napkin and some handkerchiefs. "Yep, an' I s'pose it'll be about the last time, too, Emily," she went on, sighing heavily as she straightened up and went back to her ironing. "It certainly does go hard to leave you, but a body can't live on just one wash a week, and my heart's gettin' worse every day now. Sometimes it thumps all day long. I s'pose Tom's right, an' I gotta give up work an' live with him, but it goes against the grain somethin' turrible. You know I never did like that flibbertygib of a girl he married. I druther be independent. But then that's life!"

The other woman looked distressed, Soft pink puckers came round her sweet lips.

"I'd like so much to just keep you here all the time, Becky," she said, sadly. "You know how I feel about it—but—*you know Harriet!*"

"Oh, land, yes! That could never be. Harriet an' I could never get along—that goes 'thout sayin'. But don't you worry, I know what Harriet is! You've been just wonderful to me, stickin' to me all these years, an' givin' me the wash in spite of her, an' gettin me the school-house to scrub an' all. It ain't your fault they thought I was slow. I was. I was mortal slow, but I couldn't he'p it. Some mornin's seems zif I jest couldn't drag myself along to finish, and that janitor got impatient and wanted to lock up and go home to his lunch. I couldn't blame him. I wouldda done the same in his place. But there! It's over, and what's the use talkin'?

"Harriet's gone, I s'pose, gone to her precious porch-meetin'. Well, I'm glad she's out of the house. You an' I can have a bit of a word for goodbye without her stickin' her nose in, can't we? Seem'zo I couldn't uv gone away 'thout that, I know it ain't any sweet propostition fer you, either, you poor child. Queer your pa ever took such a notion to her, leavin' the property that way, half to her. I never could make it out."

Emily flushed in a troubled way.

"Father felt under obligation," she said, hesitatingly. "Her husband was an old boyhood friend, something like you and me, you know, Becky."

The older woman flashed a look of adoration at Emily whose warm blue eyes beamed back a deep, quiet love and trust.

"Then there was some money father borrowed when he was in financial difficulty once, and lost it, and I believe he felt under obligation to look after the widow when he got in better circumstances."

"H'm! Seems zif he mighta found some way to do that that wouldn't 'a' been so hard on you!" she commented, dryly.

A puzzled pucker came between Emily's eyes:

"Father said he was thinking of me when he did it," she said, slowly. "He put it in his will that he didn't want me to be alone in the house. I think he meant it for the best. You know he was alienated from the rest of the family. They didn't have much to do with him—"

"I know! They mighta had some reason, but excuse 'em all you can they're as mean ez pusley, an' you never lost much by their bein' alienated. Your father mighta been odd. He was odd as Dick's hat-band, none odder, but he wasn't a hypocrite like most o' them, an I guess he meant well."

She shook out a towel and thumped the iron heavily over the hem.

Emily looked off with a troubled gaze.

"You see," she said, as if trying to reconcile the matter to her own satisfaction, "he'd always taken care of me in every way and he didn't realize I could look out for myself. He wanted to make sure that I would not be alone, and he figured that if she had a half right in the house she wouldn't go away and leave me. I think he meant well."

"Oh, yes" said the other woman, "I s'pose he did, an' he was right so fur as she was concerned. *She won't never go away!* She'll always freeze on to whatever's hers and stay froze. But her son, he can't get along with her, neither."

More distress in the sweet eyes.

"No," admitted Emily. "He couldn't stand being ordered round so much. And he's a good boy. He wanted to get married, but his mother wouldn't have it, said she'd never let him bring the girl he'd picked out to her house. Jud is a good boy, and that little Ariel Custer is a good girl. I'd like to see them get married; they'd be so happy!" She sighed and looked off dreamily through the kitchen-window with wistfulness in her eyes.

"Say, you look just like you did when you was a little girl!" exclaimed the older woman. "My! but you was a pretty little girl with them blue eyes—they ain't changed a mite—and them yellow curls like gold! 'Member how we useta go wading in the brook? Sometimes I think I'd like to go back and be a child again. We didn't have a care ner a pain, just blue sky and sunshine. If your mother could see you now all alone, wouldn't she take on? She never useta let you go alone anywheres, and that was my job, always to go with you. She'd pack up bread and butter, and gooseberry jam and cookies and we'd go down to the brook and wade, and play house by the hemlock-trees, with moss fer a carpet, and acorns fer cups and saucers. 'Member? I was thinkin' of it the other day. My! but the water would feel good to yer feet on a hot day now, just lappin' round yer ankles. 'Member that day when the big boys come along, and you slipped on the stone and fell in, and Nate Barrett pulled you out? I remember how your ma looked when we took you home, and how sweet she smiled at Nate, and told him she never would forget it. That was just the year before she died, wasn't it? Your pa never did like Nate, though. I remember the time Nate brought you an orange and your pa wouldn't let you have it and sent him home. It seemed real unjust after his savin' your life that way. He was a nice boy, and real fond of you."

Emily's cheeks had bloomed out rosily, but she controlled her voice steadily.

"I think father had some sort of misunderstanding with Nate's father," she apologized, bravely; "about some wood, I think it was. Father was rather quick, you know."

Emily Dillon bent her head over the apron she was mending and Rebecca Ford cast a keen glance at the brown hair that was beginning to soften with touches of silver about the edges.

"Ever hear from Nate after he went away?"

Rebecca cast the question out with a dry casualness that saved it from being embarrassing.

The pink stole higher in the softly faded cheeks and the sweet eyes clouded for an instant as their owner turned to gaze wistfully out of the window.

"No; I never heard," she answered slowly. "He went out west. That is all I know."

"Yes, he did," said Rebecca, slatting Mrs. Granniss' kimono over to make room for the towel she had just ironed, "and the other day down to the 'Merican store I heard Ike Bowman telling Dick Smith how he and his wife met up with him last winter on a trip they was taking out to Californy. You know Ike and Dick come from over Mercer way and musta known Nate. Ike said Nate was livin' on a ranch of his own, I forget whether 'twas sheep or cattle or oranges, but they said he was doin' well; had money in the bank and was well thought of, an' had a nice home. They said he looked just the same as ever, only just his hair a little gray, but his eyes looked young yet. They said he hadn't never married, an' he kep' house fer himself, but he hed everything nice, an' 'lectric lights an' water, and everything in his house. He said it was outside of some place they called Boy City or something like that. I remembered it 'cause it seemed so natural fer him to be anywhere round where there was boys. He never was much fer the girls, only you—you know—"

Emily Dillon arose suddenly and opened the door of the hall cautiously, putting her face into the opening. The breeze from the dining-room window blew on her hot cheeks and gave her steadiness as she stood apparently listening. When she turned around her face was entirely serene.

"I didn't know but Harriet had forgotten something and come back," she explained, "but I guess it was just a dog scratching at the screendoor."

Rebecca eyed her keenly with satisfaction.

"My how pretty you do look! Your cheeks is as pink as clove pinks! Your figure's as trim as when you was fourteen. That skirt's an awful good fit, I always did admire that skirt. I thought if I ever got ahead I'd get me one like it some day if you didn't mind. When you get it wore out, Em'ly, give it to me fer a keepsake. I'd like to have it hangin' round in the closet jest to remind me o' you."

"Why, you can have it now, Becky!" laughed Emily, laying down her sewing and beginning to fumble with the belt-fastening. "I'm tired of it anyway, and I don't need it. I've got two new ones. I'd love to have you wear it. There's quite a lot of wear in it yet, and I believe it would fit you. We're about of a size."

Emily unhooked her skirt and stepped out of it smiling. Rebecca Ford, iron poised in air, stood protesting delightedly.

"Oh, now Em'ly, I couldn't take it right off your back that way. I really couldn't. And you lookin' so nice in it an' all. Besides, what'll Harriet say?"

"It's not Harriet's skirt," said Emily, with dignity. "She has no call to say anything."

"Oh, well that won't stop her," declared Rebecca, wisely. "She's the most uncalled person I know, Harriet is."

Emily's eyes twinkled.

"Well, she'll never know," she soothed coaxingly, "for the other one's made almost exactly the same, pocket and all. That pocket's nice and handy too. I always like a pocket. Take it, Becky. I like to have you have it."

The other woman laid down her iron and took the coveted garment eagerly, running an admiring finger down inside the pocket.

"Land sake, Em'ly, you've left some money in here," she said, preparing to extract it.

"That's all right, Becky; keep it for good luck!"

She looked almost a girl so slim and little in her little black sateen petticoat and her neat buttoned shoes; prim and sweet and lovable. One could hardly think of her as an old maid, nor yet as even an elderly person. There were lines of youth about her, youth held in abeyance like a bud that has waited a long time to bloom.

A knock at the front door sent her scuttling up the back stairs to get another skirt, and Rebecca Ford grim and inquisitive to the hall to answer the knock. It was only a delivery wagon come to the wrong house and Rebecca quickly sent it on its way. Back in the kitchen again, she tried on the skirt and went to the dining-room side-board to get a glimpse of herself.

"Fits like the paper on the wall," she said, with a note of grim hilarity in her voice as Emily came down the back stairs again neat and trim once more in another black-serge skirt. "But I could never look like you, I stoop too much. You're straight as a pipe stem and walk like a robin. Anybody'd know me from my walk. Well, I guess I'll be wrapping it up before old Hawkeye gets back. It's near time for her to appear. What's the matter with the car? Why don't she ride in it this hot weather?"

"Well, you know she never learned to drive it herself,

and I—well I didn't feel like learning. I'm sure I should run into somebody. Besides I thought it was better not to mix things. Of course I went out in it now and then when Jud was here, but Harriet hasn't been out in it much since Jud left home."

"Where's that short-haired, outlandish Boggs girl? I thought she could always be depended on to be on tap any time when wanted."

Emily's eyes twinkled again, but she answered demurely:

"I believe she's gone to the shore with her aunt for a short time."

"H'm! Well, I thought she'd vanish when Jud went away. With all her softness, I thought Harriet would find out she wasn't so fond of just *her* as she thought. Well, Em'ly, I guess I must be gettin' along. I don't guess we'll see each other much more this side the grave. I'm not one to talk a lot, but you certainly have been a bright spot in my life. If I could just leave it here and walk out into the other, I'd be satisfied; but I do hate like pizen this next part, goin' to live with my daughter-in-law and bein' took care of. It may not last long, to be sure, and then again it may; but all I've got to say is Emily Dillon, when you get up there in your Methodist heaven just you wait around near the door for me, for you'll see me comin' long in waitin' to take care o' you. We been separated a lot these last years, but I got faith to b'lieve that the Lord that made you can save me too, and won't let us be so fur apart up there. Now, don't you look like that. If Harriet ever gets married again, or decides to live elsewhere just you let me know an' I'll come an' take care o' you again. I b'lieve 'twould cure my heart-trouble just to be gettin' your meals."

"But Becky!" cried Emily Dillon, in distress. "It's dreadful for you to be going away where you don't want to go. Just you be patient. I've always thought things would come around our way, and you keep up heart a little while longer."

Her eyes were starry with hope, and the other woman laughed wistfully:

"All right, Em'ly, you keep on havin' faith, and I'll try

to remember what you say and keep on havin' it too.
There she comes! Well, I'll say good-bye. If you ever
come Mercer-way you'll stop and see me, won't you? I
expect Tom to come after me, day after tomorrow."

The two women clasped each other's hands tensely for
a moment with tears in their eyes, while heavy steps
were coming steadily on up the walk to the front porch.
Then Emily pushed a little soft gray roll into the other
woman's hand, whispering:

"It's just a gray veil for you, Becky. I bought it the
other day. O, Becky! I shall *miss* you! You've been
almost like a mother to me many a time, and I shall *miss*
you!"

She put her hands on Rebecca Ford's shoulders and
drew her face close to hers pressing the other woman's
lips with her own in a quick, fervent kiss, and then, as
the screen-door of the hall opened, she slipped noiselessly up the back stairs to her room.

CHAPTER XIII

THE relentless footsteps came straight on to the kitch-
en, stalked about a bit; the sound of the back door key
turning in its lock, and then Harriet Granniss came up
stairs and knocked at Emily's door.

"I thought I heard some one in the kitchen as I came
in," she said, accusingly. "That lazy woman hasn't been
here all this time, has she? She had only a half dozen
pieces to iron when I left. I went and counted them.
What did you pay her? Any more than the usual
amount?"

"Oh, no," said Emily, breathing freely. "Just the usual
amount."

Harriet eyed her keenly.

"Well, if she's been here all this time she must have been ironing some of her own clothes, and using our gas and our time. They do that, you know. You've got to watch everything! I heard of a good colored woman we could get today if you weren't so sentimental about this lazy good-for-nothing. I'm sure I heard someone in the kitchen when I came in, and she hasn't ironed my kimono. She didn't put away the ironing-board, either."

Emily gave her a vague, far-away smile. She had found this the most effective mode of stopping the flow of such language which was gall and wormwood to her sweet and loving soul. It also helped her to hold in her wrath, if she could force a smile. So she smiled. There really was nothing Harriet Granniss could say to that smile, so she strode heavily into her own room and began to remove her best new voile preparatory to getting supper. It was her business to get supper that night and she always did her duty thoroughly and well, even though she often had items on her menu that she knew Emily Dillon did not eat. But then she *ought* to have liked them, and Harriet felt she was serving a good purpose when she thus forced them on her. If in return Emily had chosen to serve on her nights any article of diet which Harriet had listed as taboo, Emily would never have heard the last of it.

But tonight Emily Dillon was not thinking of menus, and she accepted a little of everything that was on the table and smiled as she listened to the town gossip from the Congregational porch-meeting. Betty Champion was going to marry Norman Hunter and take care of his seven children. An awful fool Harriet thought she was, as if women weren't better off unmarried! They said coal was going to be very scarce and high the next year or two and the Undikes were going to burn wood and nothing else. They had a fireplace in every room in the house and a lot of trees around their place. That oldest child of the postmaster's was going blind, they said; and little Nellie Smiley had run away to New York to work. There was going to be a big parade on Labor Day and she had promised to bake some devil's food for the dinner in the Borough Hall, and a rice pudding for the Poor Picnic.

Emily smiled and said "Yes," and "No" in the proper places, and ate a mincing supper, but there was a light in her eyes that made the hawk-eyed one watch her closely.

"You don't act as if you'd heard a word I said, Emily Dillon," said Harriet, unpleasantly, rising and beginning to clear away the dishes. "I declare I'd think you'd want to know a little of what was going on in the world."

"Why, yes," said Emily, pleasantly, "it's interesting, of course."

Harriet sighed ponderously. She was just aching for a fight, and Emily never would fight. Harriet was bored.

"Well, I'm going to prayer-meeting tonight!" she declared. "What about you?"

"I think I'll just stay on the porch," said Emily. "I've sort of felt the heat today."

"Well, I do my duty in spite of the heat," snapped Harriet, filling her mouth copiously from the last piece of cake on the plate, thus saving herself a trip to the cake-box.

Harriet washed her dishes noisily, and locked up the kitchen. She ascended the stairs creakingly, and put on her hat. Emily sat behind the honeysuckle-vines and watched her away in the early twilight.

It was just ten minutes to nine when a slight figure stole in at a parting of the hedge around at the side of the house and paused beside the honeysuckle end of the porch.

"Miss Emily, are you there?" whispered Ariel's soft voice.

"Yes, dear; come up and tell me all about it."

Ariel slipped under the vine and curled up by Emily Dillon's feet.

"We had a wonderful day," she said, eagerly, "and we stayed so late that I was almost afraid to come. Isn't it time for Mrs. Granniss to be home from prayer-meeting? I wouldn't come till I was sure there was no light in the house."

"She won't be home for ten minutes or so. Tell me, did you like my creek?"

"Oh, glorious! We went in a canoe all the way up to the rocks, and past the swimming-hole, and we had our dinner on a great flat rock with moss on it. There were birds singing high above our heads, and little pinecones dropped into the water down below, and there were stones with the water babbling over them!"

"O my dear! I know! I've waded there in that very spot, and fell in once—and— But tell me, did you talk about the little house and get everything all fixed up?"

There was a catch in Ariel's voice like a sob and she gripped Emily's hand that she held, in a close, convulsive fashion.

"Yes, we talked about the little house, but we didn't plan, because—well—because the thing we hoped didn't happen, and we can't buy it yet, Miss Emily. That is, we can't buy it at all, I suppose, not that one, because it's going to be sold right away. We only had the option on it till tomorrow morning at nine o'clock, because someone else is looking at it, and Mr. Packard said he positively couldn't wait another minute. But—we're going to be brave—"

"He oughtn't to run over the hour such a hot night!" declared Harriet Granniss' voice coming suddenly out of the darkness, with a clarion ring, talking to a fussy little neighbor who lived farther on. "No minister has a right to hold people in a hot room a night like this longer than is advertised. I shall tell him what I think about it the next time I see him. He was so busy with those strangers I couldn't get within ear-shot of him tonight. But it isn't right, and we ought to make him understand it."

Ariel was gone like a breath, slipping behind the honeysuckles, with a light touch of her hand on Emily's as she passed, and a mere ripple of perfume as she slid through the vines and disappeared around the house.

Harriet lumbered heavily up the steps, puffing with every breath and scanned the porch sharply.

"Is that you, Emily? Are you all alone? Didn't I hear somebody out there in the side yard? Seems to me as if I did. I suppose it was a cat, but I don't think you ought to sit out here alone when all the neighbors are gone away. Here, there wasn't a soul around this end of the street. It's all dark next door, and over to Joneses. Some day something will happen to you."

"I'm not afraid, Harriet. But now you've come, I guess I'll go to bed."

"Well, just as you please," sniffed Harriet, offendedly. She loved to have an audience after she had been out anywhere. Half the fun of going was in describing it afterward. But Emily never had cared to listen to her. "I should think you'd like to know a little about the meeting," she flung after her when she was halfway up the stairs. "You go out so little one would think you'd care to keep up with the times. But I suppose being it wasn't a Methodist prayer-meeting you don't care anything about it."

"Oh!" Emily paused and looked over the hand-rail. "Did you have a good meeting?" in her sweet, polite voice, with that low, unprovoked modulation that seemed unaware of any offense. "Were there many out? It was such a nice night."

"Yes, there were a lot out for summer considering the most important people of course are away at the seashore and mountains. But there were visitors, I'm glad to say. Two from the Inn, and three from Major Pettlebee's, and your cousin Julia Dillon. She stopped me and asked how you were, and said it was such a pity you weren't a Congregationalist like the rest of the family, so you and I could come together, and she supposed you were at your own church. I had to say no, you weren't feeling so well. So you can see how you're making me lie to save your face, Emily Dillon. For I couldn't bear to tell her you were just home sitting on your porch on a church night. Your cousin seemed real pleasant, and anxious about you. Said she wished you'd come up to-morrow and take lunch with her."

"Yes? And did your own minister speak in the meeting, or is he away on his vacation?" asked Emily, sweetly.

"Oh, he's away, but he left a real good man in his

place. I declare his talk was just heavenly. Byers' kitten came in the church and kind of upset things for a while making the Hillier twins giggle, and scooting under pews when Elder Dart tried to catch her, but the minister just gave out a hymn and never seemed to see it at all. Helena Boggs played the organ and she played it real well too. That girl is a wonder. She just got back from the seashore this afternoon, and yet she came to prayer-meeting. She's spending a couple of days with Hattie Riggs. She'll be back here tomorrow sometime. I suppose she thought maybe Jud would be there with me and she'd get a chance to see him. I can't think what that boy means acting—"

"Well, good night, Harriet, I seem to be sleepy," said Emily, and suddenly fled from the voluble tongue.

Up in her own room she pattered around in her bedroom-slippers, putting her hair in order for the night, arranging the bed-covers, reading her bit of a verse and kneeling white and still by the plump four-poster bed after the light was put out, with her small feet in a bar of moonlight on the old ingrain carpet; and then stealing softly over to the big calico-covered chair by the window.

A long time she sat there looking out into the dewy, moonlit night, in her little white home-made cambric nightgown edged with tatting, long-sleeved and buttoned up to her soft white throat just as she used to wear them long ago when her mother made them for her. The maple-tree by her window threw little flickering shadows over the wire window-screen and played over her quiet face, while she sat there far into the night, looking out. Once a little wild rabbit whisked across the grass and sat posed with ears alert and trembling nose in a splash of moonlight. Emily Dillon saw it and smiled to herself in the darkness with a happy smile. The world was still mystical with moonlight when at last she crept silently into her bed, and Harriet was noisily enjoying her rest.

"I'm going into the city this morning," Emily announced quietly enough at the breakfast-table. "Is there anything you'd like me to get for you?"

Harriet sniffed, and eyed her curiously. Wasn't that just like Emily Dillon, not to say what she was going for? Emily almost never went to the city. What on earth could she be going to do? And why didn't she ask her to go along?

"I'd thought we'd put up those tomatoes," she said discontentedly. "It's sinful to let them rot on the vines."

"Well, the tomatoes can wait. I was looking at them yesterday. It's a beautiful day and I've got my plans all made to go. I thought I'd take a little of your advice and get out."

She smiled sweetly and finished her coffee.

Harriet opened her lips to say she would go with her and then shut them with a click. No, she would never crawl after Emily Dillon for company. Emily was too close-mouthed, and she could find her own company. Very likely she was going to visit some orphan asylum or old ladies' home and take them flowers. She did that sometimes, and Harriet had no taste for such a form of amusement. A sinful waste to spend money for flowers when the heathen needed it all. She picked up her plate and carried it to the kitchen in offended silence. Emily gathered her dishes and washed them quickly in the sink, and dried them and put them away.

"Then you don't want any errands done?" she asked pleasantly.

"No, I don't!" snapped Harriet. "If I did I could do them myself. I go to the city now and then, you know."

Emily Dillon went straight to her lawyer's office in the city.

"I want you to buy a house for me," she said. "It's a little bungalow in Glenside belonging to S. S. Packard, and his telephone-number is 774 W. I think you'll find him there now. Could you call up and arrange about the purchase without his knowing who bought it?"

"Oh, yes, Miss Dillon, that can be arranged. The firm can buy it, you know. Did you wish to pay cash for it?"

"Yes, I'd like you to use some of those last bonds you bought for me. It's only a small bungalow and the price is seventy-five hundred."

"Very well, I'll call him at once."

He reached for the telephone.

"I'd like to get it all fixed up today," she said, nervously. "Could it be done as soon as that?"

"Why, if there are no complications. Possibly we could get the deed ready this afternoon. You will want the title searched of course."

"Whatever is necessary, of course, but I want the property anyway, and I want it fixed up as soon as possible. You see there are some young people who want it very much and they've had to give up the option on it because they couldn't get the money to make a payment on it. This is their address. I'd like you to write them at once, and say that your client who has purchased the bungalow understands that they have been interested in it, and that it is for rent. Then find out what they are willing to pay and rent it to them *no matter how low the rent is*. You understand, I want them to have it, no matter how little I get from it."

"I understand, Miss Dillon," said the lawyer, with a pleasant sparkle in his eyes. "I'll try to carry out your wishes."

"There's another thing, Mr. Bonsall, I'd like to make a change in my will to include this purchase."

"Certainly," said the lawyer. "I'll send for the will, and as soon as we have the details we can fix that up." He touched a button and a boy appeared. "Bring the box containing Miss Dillon's papers," he said, and went at once to the telephone.

In a few minutes more Emily Dillon was back in the city street again with the day before her. It was understood that she was to return about five o'clock to get the matter of the will fixed up. Harriet Granniss would think it very queer that she stayed away so long without explanation, but it couldn't be helped, and she felt an intense satisfaction in the thought that she was prolonging her stay not from foolish desire of her own to play around in her favorite orphan asylums and hospitals, but from a real sense of duty toward business matters. It gave her as it were a feeling that this day had just dropped down at her feet like a gift that she might do with as she pleased, and not feel any compunctions of conscience. Emily Dillon's conscience was well developed and always on the job.

She took a few steps out into the hot morning sunshine and paused wondering what she should do first. She had a vague idea in the back of her mind of doing some frivolous shopping, buying something that Harriet would consider extravagant, something that perhaps she never would really feel like wearing in Glenside—and she rarely went elsewhere. She had no definite plan other than to satisfy a craving for something beautiful that had hitherto been without the pale of things that were really necessary. She cast her eyes up and down the street, hesitating between two of the big department-stores for her first wild venture, when the label on an approaching trolley-car caught her attention. That was the car that went to Copple's Crossing! A sudden keen longing seized her to take it and spend the day in her childhood's haunts.

It was a long time since she had been in Mercer, and longer still since she had been at the old farmhouse and wandered through the fields and woods down to the Creek where she and Rebecca Ford used to play. Their talk of yesterday came back to her vividly about wading in the creek, and how delightful it would be to go there again and just see the dear old spot! If she had only thought of it in time she would have taken Rebecca, and they could have had a happy day together far from Harriet's prying eye. But it was too late to call her up for she would by this time have gone to give the last cleaning to the schoolhouse, and besides, perhaps even Rebecca with all her understanding, might think it foolish for a woman of her maturity to waste a whole day going to the woods. But there was nothing to hinder her going by herself, and no one would ever be the wiser.

She had plenty of time to go and return before five o'clock, and why should she not take this little bit of pleasuring?

With a quick little birdlike motion of determination Emily turned and went a few steps down the block to a large fancy grocery where she purchased a couple of sandwiches, a small bag of chocolates and two luscious Bartlett pears. Her heart beat rapidly as she did it, and her cheeks grew pretty and pink like a wild rose. She felt dreadfully selfish, somehow, but quite determined. She marched out joyously with her bits of packages and boarded the next car for Copple's Crossing.

It was a long ride, haltingly through the lingering city and almost endless suburbs until the wide country was reached, but Emily Dillon enjoyed every instant of it, sitting serenely with a smile on her face like her little girl self when she was allowed some unusual pleasure.

Visions of her sweet-faced mother and her faraway childhood began to come to her as she got away from the city. The wall that had been made by years of abnegation, disappointment and pain, seemed to melt away and be for the time forgotten, and her face was bright with the thoughts of happiness that might have been, some that had been, as if it were today. The smile on her face, and the dreamy look of visions in her eyes, caused more than one fellow passenger to look at her tenderly, she had so well kept her look of a little child in her maturer face, that kingdom-of-heaven look.

At Copple's Crossing there were two other passengers to get out, a man and a little boy. She was glad that she knew neither of them. She did not want to be watched nor interrupted. Some day, soon perhaps, she would go on to Mercer and look up some of her old friends. There was no real reason why she should not have done it sooner, only that Harriet would have wanted to go along and she shrank from taking Harriet into the atmosphere of things she loved, because she generally managed to spoil everything with her cynicism. But today she wanted to have all to herself. One day out of a whole lifetime to talk alone with her own soul and see some things face to face, things that she had never dared own to herself. Why should she not have it?

So she hurried on ahead with her little tripping walk, and did not even look behind at the man and boy who plodded after her. At the turn of the road she slipped between the trees and was lost to sight when the two came round the curve. She did not even know that they stood in curious wonderment to see how she had disappeared, and talked of it several times, looking back and guessing who she was.

CHAPTER XIV

UP SHE climbed by a road that was now overgrown with huckleberry and fern and laurel, and discernible as a trail only to the feet of memory. Rough branches reached out and caught at her trim little black toque, tore her veil and snatched at her prim white shirtwaist, but she climbed breathlessly, buoyantly, like one who has just drunk of the spring of youth. Her face was flushed, her toque was jostled to one side, her veil was shredded and floating triumphantly, her neat black-kid glove was split from wrist to finger where she had caught at a branch to steady herself, but she was happy, breathlessly happy, and once she laughed aloud as the underbrush caught her foot and almost threw her down. It seemed to her that she was just beginning to live.

She reached the crest of the hill, where the old chestnut-trees still stood, although a blight had struck them and there were no mossy burrs littering the ground as in the old days. She paused to look up and remember Nate Barrett's smiling face as it looked that day he climbed the tree to shake down more nuts for her. It was almost as if his spirit had come back, too, to wander with her in their old haunts, where they had not met since the day her angry father threw his gift of an orange in his face and ordered him from the porch. She had thought, then, that her life was ended, and for many long nights her pillow had been wet with bitter tears; but submission and patience had wrought their sweet work in her heart and taken the sting from her trouble. Nate Barrett knew it was not her fault. He had been young then, very young, with all his way to make in the world, and she scarcely more than a child, though even then keeping house for her father who had never loved her enough to keep from drinking and disgracing her. There had never been any lovemaking between them before the episode of the orange, only good comradeship. But when her father threw that luscious orange straight into his face with a drunken force that sent its rich juice smashing through the golden rind, Nathan Barrett stood still, wiped the drops from his forehead, and looked the angry man straight in the face:

"My father was just as good as you are, Jake Dillon, and my family have always been honorable and clean if they weren't high and mighty. I can't do anything about it now; but believe me, I'm going to show you that I'm good enough to associate with your daughter, if she *is* the finest of the fine, and *don't you forget it!*" Then turning to the distressed girl, he had said: "Emily, there'll never be anybody like you in my life, and I guess you know that, though I've not said such a word to you before. I'm going away and I'm going to be somebody you won't be ashamed of, and if you ever feel free you have just to let me know, for I'll always be waiting for you."

Then he had turned on his heel and gone down the path to the gate, head up, shoulders square and determined, and gone out of her life. The years had come and gone, full of homely duties and monotony, full of angry complaining from her father, and sprees that grew longer and closer together, full of a steady attempt on her part to be a good daughter and fulfil the last request of her dying mother, "Take care of father, mother's little girl. You know he needs it." Her one comfort had been that Nathan knew of her promise whispered into the dying ear, and Nathan would not expect her to leave her post of duty. But *why* in all the years had Nathan never written? That question had troubled her for years, because she had felt sure that he would have found a way to communicate if he had tried. And yet, perhaps he would not feel it honorable after having been forbidden by her father to have anything to do with her. And of course in all that time he might have changed. He might have forgotten. Men were that way, people told her. She had no intimate knowledge of such things herself, save as she judged by her father. So the raw sorrow had burned itself into her soul and purified her until submission had come to smooth the pain away and bring the peace and the young look back into her eyes. As she grew older and saw the sorrows of some of her young companions, married to the young men of their choice but many of them cast aside after a few months or years like an old coat, or tortured by neglect, or actually sinned against, having to toil too hard and receiving nothing in return but hard words and cruel treatment, she came to think her lot was tolerable, even lovely in comparison. For had she not Nate's word that she was all in all to him, that there would never be another in his life? True, he had been only a boy and he might have changed, but as she did not know it, why torment herself by thinking so? He had never written. His mother and he had dropped as it were out of the universe. Perhaps he was dead. That had been her thought. But still she had life, and love had been hers, a love that she might keep forever bright and clear in her heart. And so she had endured and made her desert blossom with loveliness because of that brief sweet, hurried word he had said at parting.

The years had gone, and her father had lived most miraculously long, considering how he had imposed upon his physique. A strong, hard, wiry old man, making it hard for everybody with whom he came in contact, yet having his virtues, too, that would crop out in erratic ways like putting Harriet Granniss for life into his daughter's home without consulting her. Perhaps he did it for love. Emily tried to think so, and tried to forget his hardness now that he was gone.

Once she had thought that perhaps if Nathan was anywhere in her world he would hear of her father's death and come to see her, but five long years had passed, and no word had been heard of Nathan, and now she had settled it in her mind that he was either dead, or had forgotten, or perhaps he thought it was too late.

Then, yesterday, out of a clear sky, had come Becky's quiet gossip. Nathan was alive! He had been seen and talked with by residents of Glenside. He had succeeded; and he was still unmarried! He had set up a home by himself! Amazing facts! Ever since she had heard them and felt the clutch of her heart and the leap of the blood into her cheek she had wanted to get away and think. Her quiet, midnight chamber had not been quiet enough for her to dare to really take out the sacred past and search into the innermost recesses of her heart. Somehow the walls would cry out to Harriet and make her know if she thought about it at home. The very wallpaper would reveal to those prying eyes that her housemate had a secret, and presently Harriet would propound some bald and piercing question that would throw a horrible searchlight into her brain and Harriet would just pick out what she wanted and crow over it and sneer about it, and Emily would be *done*. She felt that she could never live if that happened. And so she had come to this quiet childhood haunt to take out her soul and look into her past.

She skirted the old farm, going across the high bridge. In the distance she could see Ephraim Sears, its present owner, and Silas Hawkins the hired man pitching hay on the hay-wagon—probably the same old hay-wagon where she had ridden and played as a child. Everything about the old farm was well cared for, well preserved. And yet—what nonsense! It was years and years. She was forty-two! Twelve from forty-two—she must have been twelve the last time she rode on the hay-wagon. Thirty years! Could a wagon live so long? Its lines were archaic against the horizon. It might be. But—could *love* live so long? Yet it had lived in her heart. At least the idea of it had lived. She could see the strong, fine lines of the boyish figure now as he stood with one hand on the gate and told her there would never be anyone else in his life to take her place, and it still made her heart thrill to think of it! But he would have changed. He must have changed, as she had. He would be fat and gray-haired, and different, perhaps. Other men were. There was Dill Foster, slouchy and grouchy, nothing at all like the slim, elegant youth he used to be. There was Joe Freeman, fat and red and a fool with women, instead of the fresh-faced smiling boy she remembered. Undoubtedly Nate would have changed. She had changed herself. She was an old woman. Old! old! old! She tried to rub it into her consciousness, but in spite of her the wind blew the idea away and the birds laughed at her in a joyous song. She wasn't really thinking those thoughts at all, and she knew she wasn't, as she tripped along over the bridge, the same old bridge over which she used to go to school when Nate, carrying her books, walked beside her. Nate's spirit wouldn't have changed—hers hadn't. She was the same little girl in a blue gingham dress to herself. It was her spirit that stayed young and still wore blue gingham. Her eyes would be able to see the young spirit of Nate and he would see her that way. They had always been able to look into each other's spirits. That was what had made it possible for her to live all these lonely years without him, doing her duty and just waiting.

The men in the hay-field had stopped their work and were watching her. Si Hawkins was pointing to her, and Ephraim Sears had turned clear around and rested on his pitchfork-handle. She hastened her steps and slipped into the woods. It was no part of her plan to be recognized.

Down near the old swimming-hole she found the flat rock where they used to eat their picnic-lunches so long ago, and here she spread her tiny feast. She ate with relish and leisure, recalling faces long since gone, and jokes that she had not thought of for years; and always one face, and one voice that rose above them all.

After her meal was finished she swung herself timorously down the steepness till she came to the little path close to the water. It was overgrown with tangled weeds and flowers, but still there must be children's feet which now and then traveled that way, for there was a path distinct beneath the overgrowth. It was a bit hard traveling, and she found her knees trembling, but more perhaps from excitement than fatigue. She told herself with a smile that Harriet would have made a great fuss about her doing it, and would have prophesied rheumatism and broken limbs, and all sorts of evils to follow. But this was Emily's day, and she meant to have everything belonging to it.

She wandered up a little way above the swimming-hole where the water was shallower and where they used to wade and cross on stepping-stones. There she sat down again, dreamily watching the little stream babble by her, rippling around the stepping-stones that still lifted their heads above the water here and there. Perhaps not the very same stones, but more stones like them, and here as she looked there came a small procession of little bare feet of other days, and little gathered-up gingham skirts, laughing faces, flying curls, merry shouts, boys' voices gruff and deep; and one voice—always one voice above them all.

By and by, led by an unquenchable longing, she stooped with reddening cheeks, half ashamed of herself, unfastened her neat, laced boots, and took them off. The cool breeze on her slim, stockinged foot gave a little thrill of shock, but she persevered. With a timid glance about and up where a saucy robin eyed her from a lofty perch, she unfastened her immaculate white stockings and slipped them off, sliding the whiteness of her feet beneath the black-serge skirt that was just a little too long for the modern fashion.

For several minutes she sat thus, huddled on the stone, her feet deliciously cool against the lushness of the wild grass, and the velvet of the moss. Somehow now she had done it her age and station rose about her to shame her, and she half thought she heard a stir amid the tall grass and wild yellow daisies on the opposite bank. But the sweet air moved about her soothingly, a bee sang drowsily, a bird caroled joyously far up, and the place grew still—still and alone, so after a little while she gathered courage and arose. She ventured cautiously down to the brink, her black skirts lifted, her little white feet gleaming like a child's, and stepped out, with many hesitations, stepped out upon the first stepping-stone, and stood, poised like a small blue heron, on one little foot with the other tucked up almost out of sight. Then she put the other down on the next stone, a lower one, and the water laughed and ran over it in soft tickley ripples, and little cool stings. She laughed aloud herself and took another step, this time a slippery one, and farther, and she drew her breath quickly and paused to get her balance. How mortifying if she should fall in and have to go home wet! And Harriet— But she would *never* go home that way. She would stay in the woods till she dried. Not even for the fear of pneumonia would she go home and face Harriet's consternation and contempt. She could hear the sharp, keen voice like a knife now cutting through the air:

"You! A woman of forty-five!" Harriet always anticipated one's age by a few measures. "*You!* a grown-up woman! to go wading like a child! Emily Dillon, you must be simple-minded! I always said you needed a nurse! No wonder your father left it in his will that I was to take care of you!"

Just like that she would say it! Harriet always managed to get that will in somehow when she was angry with her. Emily's cheeks burned hotly with indignation, and she steadied herself with resolution. She would not fall in and she would not ever let Harriet know that she had gone wading. That should be a sealed secret between herself and the woods as long as she lived. She was here today to have a happy time, and no Harriet should hinder.

So she went all the way across, slowly, joyously, remembering how Nathan Barrett had walked beside her the first time and held her hand still she was used to balancing alone on the slippery stones. It was as if he walked beside her now in all his young strength, and steadied her timid feet, and there was a light of wonder and delight in her eyes as she lifted them to the billowy clouds in the blue sky over the distant hay-fields. Something was growing in her, an idea, vague and unformed, but so great and so breathless that she dared not entertain it till she was safe on dry land. Slowly, cautiously, she crept back again to her big stone, and dried her little white feet with her handkerchief; dried them quickly, surreptitiously, and slid them furtively into the stockings.

It was just as she started to put on one shoe that she heard a step somewhere, across on the other bank, and a rustle and crack of twigs. She stopped short, with her hands at her shoe, her breath held and that rigidness of form that a squirrel takes on a branch when someone approaches. An instant she held her breath, and then turned her glance across the stream without even lifting her lashes. There was no sign of anyone. It might have been a heron, perhaps, or a chipmunk, yet it sounded like a step. In panic she hurried on her shoes and laced them with trembling fingers. Some time after, she heard another movement of the tall grass farther away toward the farm. She listened awhile, and then stole away up higher into the deep of the woods out of sight on a mossy bank at the roots of great hemlocks that bent and dipped till their lacy branches reached the water and dimpled it now and then with a caress as it passed. Here she sat a long time watching the drifting lights and shadows as they sifted down around her through the lacy branches, lights reflected from the water or coming from the sun above, but soft and flickering and mysterious, like spirit-sunshine in a world of souls. And here, alone amid the green quiet of the woods with the little brook seeping, rippling happily below, a bee humming drowsily in the flowers across the bank, and the distant sound of scythes in the hay-field over on the farm she thought out her idea and made her real plan. Somehow here it seemed as though God were with her giving her courage to see things as they really were, with no silly barriers of her world that had held her in prison so long. She was thinking out a destiny and she was not afraid to call her soul her own.

She did not go back by way of the bridge. She had too great a consciousness of the farmer and his helper, and now that she had come to her decision she did not want to meet anyone or have the beauty of her day dispelled. Besides, there was barely time to get back to her appointment before the office would be closed. So she climbed the hill higher, and went down on the other side to the Pike that met the trolley farther on. She had to cross three fields, and hurried a good deal, trembling and breathless with the exertion and flushed with the heat, but she reached the trolley just in time. All the way into the city, she sat hugging herself with delight at what she had done, and at what she had decided to do. It was as if she looked at the details of the road, as she passed, with new eyes.

CHAPTER XV

IT WAS half past six when Emily Dillon entered the door, and Harriet Granniss was just sitting down to a solitary meal.

"Well, you decided to come home at last, did you?" she said, with an acrid smile. "It is a wonder you didn't take dinner in town somewhere and make an evening of it."

Emily Dillon smiled without the usual meek apology in her face.

"I was detained," she said, in a business-like tone. "I expected to make the five-thirty. I am sorry to have held back supper, but I had just time to get on this train without waiting to phone for you to go on and eat. I wish you would never wait for me when I am late."

"Well, everything's stone cold by this time," Harriet answered, haughtily. "Perhaps you enjoy cold muffins; I don't! But I'm not one to sit down and gorge myself alone. Of course if you prefer cold meals to hot ones I'll have to take them too. You speak as if you intended to make a practice of coming home late after this."

"Well perhaps I shall," smiled Emily, putting her toque on a chair and sitting down at the table. "What beautiful muffins! And you've made some orange marmalade. I'm really very hungry, and it all looks so good."

Harriet Granniss gradually grew more mollified and attempted to find out what Emily had been doing all day, but though she threw out every kind of an opening short of actually asking her pointblank, which she never could bring herself to do, Emily smiled and kept her own counsel. After supper Emily did the dishes and then went out on the porch and sat for an hour conversing with Harriet about the things she knew she liked to talk of: what kind of a suit Harriet would get for winter; how she would make over her last winter's purple tricotine, and whether it was really best to wash woolens in hot water or lukewarm; also whether the nextdoor neighbors lived as happily as they seemed to do, and whether the postmaster ever read letters. There was some gossip about a young girl who was pretty and wild; a slur about the Methodist minister, and a tale that a woman on the next street had wine on her table every day in spite of prohibition, and had been seen in her car drunk several times, to which Emily would not condescend; but she managed to mollify Harriet with descriptions of winter coats she had seen in the shop-windows, until finally she said good night with less than her usual stiffness, and they parted at the top of the stairs and went to their rooms.

Emily did not go to her bed immediately, tired though she was from her unusual day. Instead, she fussed over her immaculate bureau-drawers for awhile, laid out some clean garments for the morning, and sat long by her little desk going over papers, some of which she destroyed. The neighbor across the way told Harriet the next day that she should think they'd have a big electric-light bill, for she saw a light in Miss Dillon's room at two o'clock when she got up to give Johnny his medicine.

But there was nothing about Emily Dillon's face the next morning at breakfast to show that she had sat up late the night before. On the contrary, she looked serene as a summer morning and took all Harriet's gibes with a good-natured smile.

"Well, I s'pose you're going a-gadding again today," snapped Harriet, setting down the coffeepot and letting her ample proportions into her chair carefully. "This is your day to go up to your bank with your check, isn't it? It's come, hasn't it?" and she nodded inquiringly toward the long envelope that lay by Emily's plate along with the weekly *Methodist Review* and a begging letter from her pet orphan asylum.

"Yes, it's come," said Emily, indifferently, laying the letter by itself.

"Well, I s'pose those tomatoes'll have to wait till you come back, for I'm not going to do them alone. For mercy's sake hurry back! I don't see why you can't be reasonable and bank in Glenside. I'm sure if it's good enough for me it ought to be good enough for you."

"Well, you know Harriet, I like to stick to the old bank where father always went," soothed Emily, tasting her coffee delicately like a bird.

"Oh, yes, I know you're hidebound. You can't ever do anything but what you've always done."

Emily smiled at some inner thought.

"Now you'll just waste this whole day. I know you. You'll forget all about the tomatoes—"

Emily looked troubled for a moment.

"I'm sorry about the tomatoes, Harriet, but suppose we don't put them up this year. Neither of us likes them put up anyway. I don't really know why we grow them. I suggest that you pick them and give them to your friends."

Harriet arose from the table in wrath and gave Emily the benefit of her most withering glance.

"That's just like your easy ways, Emily Dillon! Give away perfectly good vegetables that we have and don't cost us anything! Give them away when we ought to put them up just as everybody else does. We have them in our garden and it's a sin to let them go to waste! Give them away! H'm!"

"But why have them in our garden?" questioned Emily, mildly. "You know you don't like stewed tomatoes, Harriet. And I never eat them."

"I consider it my duty to eat everything that is set on the table. Whatever *you* do, I always do my duty," declared Harriet, severely. "The Bible says that there is nothing common nor unclean, and I can eat tomatoes or anything else that grows, even if I don't like them. I'm not a slave to my dislikes as you are. And as for the garden, I'd be ashamed to say I hadn't any tomatoes in mine. Why *every*-body grows tomatoes *of course!*" She marched from the room with a gathering of soiled dishes and thumped them down in the sink. Emily carried hers and washed them as usual, without a word; and then, gathering up her mail, went to her room.

In a few minutes she came down with her little black toque and veil on, and stopped in the kitchen-door while she buttoned her glove.

"Well, good-bye, Harriet, I want to catch this next car," she said, amiably. "I'm sorry about the tomatoes, but that's really the way I feel about them." She lingered with a wistful look at the belligerent back of her house mate, but no answer came from the hard-shut lips and she turned away saying again: "Well, good-bye, Harriet. Don't wait for me if it comes time to eat."

And then she was gone down the little flower-bordered walk, out the ornate pillared gate, past the neatly trimmed hedge, down the street to her trolley.

Harriet Granniss waited until she heard the front gate click, and then she put on an old sunbonnet that she kept for aggressive purposes and went out in the garden to pick tomatoes. She picked and picked in the sweltering sun, great red, luscious, ripe, overgrown fruit, till her back ached, her knees trembled, and her eyes began to have spasms of red and green. She filled all the pans and baskets she could find, and then she emptied some of them on the kitchen table and began to pick some more. She picked even the green ones—every tomato on the patch. She stripped the vines clean, and then she pulled them up and put them in a desolate, subdued pile down at the end of the lot and left the garden with a great bare square where the flourishing vines had been, the pride of her heart and the admiration of the neighborhood. Emily Dillon should see!

She went in the house and hung up the sunbonnet sitting down heavily in a kitchen chair with the perspiration streaming down her red face, and there she sat puffing and glaring at the tomatoes, red and green. In her green-and-white checked gingham dress she strongly resembled an overgrown tomato herself at that moment. When she had sufficiently recovered her equilibrium she arose and made a cup of strong coffee, then she put on the teakettle and got out the preserving-kettle. There was a look about her mouth that boded no good for those tomatoes. She swathed herself in an immense apron and rolled around the kitchen noisily and efficiently, preparing glass jars, hunting rings and tops, filling the salt-jar and the kitchen sugar-bowl, getting out her mother's receipt-book which always figured at a time like this, more particularly as it contained receipts which were not common in the Dillon annals, nor much favored by Emily. Harriet was in a continual state of endeavoring to force Emily into liking what she liked and had always been accustomed to. The effort was all the more aggravating to Harriet because Emily always accepted the result so cheerfully and patiently, striving to say something nice about it even when one could see she didn't care for it.

Harriet wrought with knife and fire and glass jars until far beyond the usual lunch hour, momently expecting the arrival of Emily, and telling herself that if Emily would go off when there was extra work to be done she must just expect to wait for her lunch, that was all. But Emily did not come. Harriet concluded not to stop for any lunch herself, and went on her heroic way, wearing a martyr-like air and glancing at the thermometer to note with satisfaction that it was running higher than any day so far that week. When the red tomatoes were all stowed away behind shining glass and standing in neat and orderly rows, labeled and ready to put away, she began to make pickles with all her might. She cut and chopped and cooked. She used up vinegar and spices and celery-seed. Twice she had to call up on the telephone and have things sent up from the grocery-store to aid in the scheme of pickling which had grown through the day into vast proportions. The day wore slowly on, and the last tomato was screwed down under the last jar-top, the jar wiped and set at the end of the row with its severe little label "Piccalilly" on its front. The task was done. Emily could say no more about the tomatoes. They were saved and ready for anything.

Harriet glared at the clock. She was weary almost to exhaustion, and there was no dinner. It was ten minutes to six, and in fifteen minutes the train would come in, the train on which the gadding Emily would likely arrive, the same train she came on the night before. Harriet shut her thin lips tight and made a resolve. If Emily wanted dinner that night she might get it herself. No dinner would be got by her in that house that night after the herculean task she had accomplished. She would make a pitcher of iced tea, and take it upstairs with some bread and butter and orange marmalade. Then she could take a bath and be in bed when Emily came if she hurried. She strode around that kitchen with a vigor that was surprising after all she had done all day, and while the kettle was boiling she gathered her bread and butter, the left-over wing of a chicken, a bit of raisin cake, and her cup and plate on a tray. Without her usual fear of waste she cut a good sized chunk of ice and put it in her pitcher of tea. Who had a better right after her hard day's work? And hastily cutting a lemon she seized the sugar-bowl and made good her way to the second floor just as the town clock was striking six.

She stowed her provender in her bedroom, took a hasty sponge off in the bathroom, and was just getting into her night-gown when the six-five steamed into Glenside. She settled herself on her pillow with her supper under the bed out of sight, and a palm-leaf fan for attendant. Emily should get the full benefit of her deed of desertion. She was glad that she always kept the aromatic ammonia handy on her bedside-table. It would show Emily. For really, now she was down on the big, cool bed she felt as if maybe she might be going to die, she was so tired, and the blood in her head seemed about to burst out, it throbbed so hard. How she ached! How furious she was at Emily, to go off all day and have a good time and leave her to do all that work! Her blood boiled higher and hotter as she lay there fanning and waiting for the sound of Emily's footstep down in the hall. But the minutes went by and no Emily came.

CHAPTER XVI

THREE days later the Glenside fire-whistle sounded such a blast as drove the peaceful inhabitants of the little borough out of their houses and into the street, or to their various windows. All those who could, ran with all their might toward the fire-house. Those who could not run waited to hear which way the engine would take before starting to follow, but no engine went clattering out, as it usually did after an alarm like that, and yet the alarm continued to sound and screech the louder. For a half hour it sounded, and then gradually the word drifted about that someone was lost, a child probably. Excitement rose high, and every one began to count and locate his children. At last came a lame man with a white, important look.

"Heard who was lost? Emily Dillon! Been gone for three days and no one don't know where she's at! They got a posse out scourin' the woods, an' they're talkin' of bloodhounds an' the State constabulary if they don't find her before dark, poor soul!"

"Emily Dillon! Why! How? What?"

"Getting kind of queer, I suppose," supplied the old man, sadly shaking his head. He liked to think Emily Dillon was getting old and queer, for once in her younger days she had turned him down rather neatly in favor of a younger boy. "I understand it isn't the first time it's happened," he embellished his story once more.

"You don't say! Why, I never should have thought it! Why, I met Emily Dillon only day before yesterday."

"Well, she's *gone!*" he rolled the words as a sweet morsel under his tongue. "Yes, she is gone, and they're very much afraid of *foul play!*"

He whispered the last two words hoarsely.

"Oh, you don't mean it!"

"Yes that's what I hear. Well, I must be getting on. Seems queer, don't it, to have a real tragedy happen right here in our little town; well, you never can tell, you never can tell, what's gonta be the outcome of a day."

Husbands came home on the evening trains, heard the tale with wise, doubting eyes and half amused smiles.

"Oh, she's off visiting somewhere, you may depend, and when she gets good and ready she'll turn up. Foul play! Nonsense! As if anything like that could happen in this quiet little town with a perfectly good police force and several plain-clothes men on the alert all the time. No, you'll see Miss Dillon back again among us before very long and don't you forget it! I've heard she's none too happy with that Granniss family in the house. There's been some trouble there. The son's left home. Probably he and Miss Dillon didn't agree. You mark my words, *she's* not lost."

The night came down and the boys of the town hurried into old army-trousers and ancient sweaters, and went out with alacrity to search the woods. Men telephoned home from the drugstore that they wouldn't be back for awhile, they were going to stay up and help pump the quarry dry. They were dragging the quarry pond for her body! Women shivered in their sheltered homes and went in early from their cool porches. They couldn't seem to bear the leafy shadows of the lawn. It made them think of dark shapes all dripping, with clinging skirts and draggled hair. The word "suicide" was whispered softly over shadowed gateways, and behind the hedges. Wasn't it a pity! She always seemed so sweet and quiet!

The night wore on, the quarry-hole was pumped dry, and still no clue. A detective arrived on the scene in the morning, and the alienated relatives woke up and began to ask about that will, and what had become of Jud Granniss? There was talk, too, of Ariel Custer, and shakings of heads.

"Too bad! I always thought he wasn't good enough for her. But that's what comes to girls without mothers, having to make their way in the world. Any man can turn their heads. Jus' so he's a man!"

The talk drifted to the machine-shop where Judson Granniss had found a temporary job, because it paid better than his old position in the city. He had been in the city the night before and gone early to his job in the morning, and so had not yet heard of the excitement. He heard the gossip going around, asked a few direct questions then dropped his tools and went to his mother.

Harriet Granniss, stolid, indignant, frightened and belligerent but dominant as ever, met her son's anxious glance without flinching. She was not going to make friends with him easily just because there was trouble, unless she found he was ready to give in to her will.

"So you thought you'd come around and get a finger in the pie!" she sneered. "Have you come to find fault or give advice?"

"Mother! This is serious business!"

"Well, I guess I wasn't born yesterday!" she came back. "Did you s'pose that was news to me? But anyway, whatever happens, this house belongs to me!"

"If I were you I wouldn't say anything about that now, Mother; it may make things look queer for—us—you know!"

"Oh! Us! US!" she screamed. "I suppose you mean

yourself and that silly girl. I suppose you're afraid A—e—riel won't marry you if there's any talk about us, she's so aristocratic!"

The young man's nostrils quivered angrily and his lips were white, but he controlled himself.

"Leave Ariel out of the question, please, Mother."

"Leave Ariel out! You weren't so ready to leave her out last week! You'll find she won't get left out if we get into it and it gets into the papers! You'll find your fine lady will be smirched as well as the rest of us. You'll find they will ask if you know anything about Emily Dillon. And how do I know but you do? You two were always so thick!"

"Mother, will you be sensible?" The young man was controlling himself by the hardest effort. "We need to talk this thing over calmly and advise together."

"Oh, *advise!* No! I don't need your advice, thank you," she said, bitterly. "I haven't quite come to that pass, thank fortune! I still have my senses and can order my own course. If you are going to stick to that silly, yellow-haired girl you can *get out of my house!*"

Down in the village various theories had been advanced. It was known that Emily Dillon had last been seen at the corner waiting for the trolley to take her to Bolton, a little old town halfway between Glenside and Mercer, where her father had always banked and where she had continued to put certain portions of her income, rather because she enjoyed the excuse for the ride and the occasional meeting with old acquaintances than because of any sentimental reason. Perhaps, too, partly because she didn't care to have Glenside know all her affairs. She had talked with Abe Morse, "passed the time of day," said how pleasant the weather had been since the last rain, and asked after Amy Morse's baby. The town took a satisfaction in repeating over from neighbor to neighbor the common, homely phrases that savored of every day, and had no hint of dreary quarry-holes, and masked men by midnight. It was known that she had taken the car for Bolton for Abe Morse helped her on, and said she smiled good-bye and told him not to stand too long in the hot sun, it was bad for him.

"Kind, always *kind* and thoughtful, Emily was," he murmured.

"Is!" sharply asserted his wife, who was a good friend of Emily's. "I'll *never* believe she committed suicide. That's rank nonsense! What would she want to commit suicide for, now when she's just got her own way in life for the first time since she was born?"

"Well, they do say," said Abe, lowering his breath, "that she ain't so happy with Harriet Granniss. Harriet won't have this, and will have that, till Emily don't know she owns her own soul. She's been druv to the back room in a house that should by good rights belong entirely to Emily. I was a good friend of Jake Dillon, but I do say that he did wrong by her when he set her shoulder to shoulder with that she-devil."

"Now, Abe!" broke in his wife; "I'm surprised at you. Harriet Granniss may not be as pleasant to live with as some, but she's a good woman, we all know that, and she's a member in good and regular standing—"

"Good and reg'ler standing ROT! What's that got to do with it? There's hypocrites in all churches and before this thing's cleared up we'll know who a few of them are, or I'll miss my guess! Hannah, now answer me this: Do you know who would get that house if it was proved that Emily Dillon's dead? Do you *know?* Well I *thought* you didn't. *Harriet Granniss* would! That's who! Now, what do you think?"

"But—"

"No buts about it, and do you know what they're sayin'? Well they're sayin' that Harriet Granniss and her precious son, and mebbe that wild girl with the short hair knows more'n they want to tell about where Emily Dillon is."

The city papers made much of the matter in little paragraphs with black-letter headings on the front page, and Glenside came into immediate prominence. There was even an editorial about "making our suburbs safer" with the Glenside "Abduction" as illustration of "what we have come to in these days." Every morning the paragraph appeared with new embellishments, as for instance:

"State-wide search is being made for the body of Miss Emily Dillon, an elderly matron of Glenside who wandered away, three days since, from her home in the absence of her attendant for a few minutes, and has not as yet been found. It is feared that she has met with foul play as she carried quite a sum of money upon her person. Miss Dillon belongs to an old and respected family in the County, being directly descended from the Dillons of Mercer, and great anxiety is felt among her kinsmen. A cousin, Dalton Dillon of Hilton Heights, is strong in the belief that she has met with foul play and declares his intention of tracing this to the source and punishing the criminal. He hints at clues that are being traced, and revelations that will soon be made."

The news was copied in the county papers and drifted over to Mercer the day after Emily's disappearance had been made public. Ephraim Sears and Si Hawkins nodded their heads over it, and winked at the supper-table.

"That was *her*, Si," whispered Joe, when his wife went to the pantry for more bread. "I thought I couldn't be mistaken, though I ain't seen her fer years. Best keep yer mouth shet awhile an' yer eyes open. She might be round here yet somewheres, and there'll likely be a reward. Where there's money there's always a reward, you know."

CHAPTER XVII

Down by Copple's Creek the weeds grew thick and rank, spangled themselves with golden, starry blossoms that in the evening made pale moons in groups and clusters, and lit the way along the limpid water by reflection. The old moon rose, and shed its thin radiance, lying on its back and looking down as it were over the edge of its couch, throwing lacy lights on the old swimming-hole through the fingers of the hemlocks.

Quite early in the evening, just after dark, a small shadowy figure stole from the road and threaded a shy way up among the trees, over the ridge and down among the purples and blacks of the wooded hills. Stealing stealthily on tired feet; cautiously, waiting now and then to listen; alert at the sound of a falling nut or a stirring bird, or a little black bat on wing. Veiled and neat and shy, she went steadily forward, feeling her way as if by some inner sense because most of the woods were black as velvet, and only the tinkle of the water far down in the ravine to guide. Going so she came at last to the shallows and the stepping-stones just a little above the swimming-hole, stepped softly down and paused. The night was still and soothing. When she looked up the old moon seemed to smile with its thin, gray lips as if to say: "You and me—you and me too, old comrade!" and the stars gave a far-away twinkle as if they understood.

How long she stood there by the brink with the soft little swish of the water in the grass at her feet and the occasional Tchug! of a bullfrog under the dipping roots of the old tree by her side, she did not know. But as she stood she seemed to see in panorama against the cool green dusk of the night, all the scenes of her childhood, the faces of those she had loved; and all the things which had hurt her and oppressed her for months and years seemd to fall away like a burden and leave her light and happy. The longer she stood the more she seemed to feel herself in rhythm with the passing water, so still, so sweet, so cool, slipping, slipping by, and to feel its old-time power over her body, and its call to her to come. If only she might be a boat and lie on its smooth surface rocking and floating, with her hands folded and her tired head resting back on the cool pillow. Her body felt so light she was sure it would float. A crazy thought, of course, but she toyed with it, so light she seemed, so good and cool the water would feel. The pull of the little stream was so strong that suddenly she sat down where she was and clutched at the bank as if some enemy were drawing her against her will. Then feeling safer she drew her veil away from her white, tired face and dipping her hand in the water, passed it over her forehead. Her hot, hot forehead! Ah! How good it felt! How good it would feel to be wet all over! She stooped and dipped her arms in up to the elbow, pushing higher and higher the stiff black reluctant sleeves. Once she slipped as she stopped and one foot went into the water and found a footing on a broad wet stone. The water stole into her shoe, and was cool and delightful. She stood up cautiously and stepped out ankle deep. There was something about the heat of the day and the lure of the stream like a drunken man in front of whiskey. The more she felt the more she longed for its coolness. With a stealthy glance around she stepped farther, and sat slowly down, her hands out on either side to steady her, her heart beating wild with a childish joy. The water lapped up to meet her poor hot limbs, touching with a soothing peace her fevered veins. How good it was! Of course she was getting her skirt wet, her good skirt! but then, it would dry by morning! And anyhow, what did it matter?

As the coolness stole upon her and her weariness and excitement increased, she fancied herself a child again playing by the creek. She lifted her dripping hands and dabbled her face again with their coolness; and then following an irresistible impulse, she lay down. Ah! This was heaven, though it frightened her for a bit.

But the water was not deep enough here to cover her face. She lay back with her head on a big flat stone, to let the coolness and peace steal upon her, and the soft touches of the water take the ache from her tired joints. She could look up and see the stars, as if they were twinkling and chuckling with her over what a trick a staid woman like her was carrying through all alone in the night. There was one other in the whole world besides the stars that she knew would understand, perhaps sometime either in this world or the next she would tell and they would laugh together.

Presently as she lay there rocking with the softly moving water, she found that by touching the tips of her fingers lightly to the stones on either side she could make her body lift a tiny bit and float, and oh, it was so restful, like an air pillow she had tried once. A water bed! Where had she heard that phrase? It was something they used in the hospital for people with hurt spines. Well, she was lying on a water bed, and it was like going to heaven "on downy beds of ease," the way they used to sing in prayer-meeting when she was a little girl, "while others fought to win the prize and sailed through bloody seas!" finished out the old hymn in her ears. Well, she had sailed enough red seas with no prizes at the end either, and maybe it was all right for her to have this one bit of ease. She knew in the back of her mind it was crazy, but it was good and she did not feel ashamed of doing it.

Into the midst of her dreamy imaginings came a soft sound, hardly definable, chug, chug, chug, breaking into the lethargy that was stealing over her, and bringing her alertly to a realization of her strange position.

The noise was distinct now, the quick padding of heavily tired wheels, an automobile going over rough ground and seemingly coming straight toward her. She rose from the water in horror with starting eyes across the stream, but the moon-faced blossoms, huddled starrily, gazed back at her serenely. Perhaps she was dreaming.

The car seemed to have stopped beyond the clump of willows, and there were subdued voices, and the word "Now!" quite distinctly. Then the sound of a heavy body splashing into the water; a dull thud, an almost imperceptible gasp of nature, as if the clear little stream were resenting the entrance of the unknown, then the soft purr of the starting engine, backing, backing, and flying away in the distance. The water seemed to draw breath and move in relief upon its way again.

Back by the stepping-stones the little alert figure relaxed with a sigh into the water once more. It was comforting and friendly after her fright. She closed her eyes and wondered what had fallen into the stream and a shudder passed over her. She drew down her veil and fastened it tight to keep out the starlight and bring back the pleasant dreams. Putting down her hands on the stony bottom again she began lifting and rocking herself like a little child. She could feel the current moving by her, and when she let her body go it drew her with it to arm's length, then she pulled herself back again. She began to shift her hands and let her body go farther.

The ache in her back and limbs was all gone now and her thirsty, fevered body was drinking up new life. She felt like the little boat she had imagined, as with her fingertips on the bottom she drifted farther and farther down the stream. By the gurgle all about her she knew she must have reached the miniature rapids now. She could feel the current stronger and sweeter, drawing her as if it loved her, saying, "Come with us and we will do you good?"

Her mind was keen and alert as she lay and listened to the wooing of the water. She must be nearing the tiny narrows the only spot where a canoe could get through the rapids. It would be delicious to float through there and feel herself carried along without effort of her own. After that she would stop, pull herself back, and get out. It was late and she must be getting dry before the morning. She had heard the old bell in the Mercer church-tower sounding out two clear strokes shortly before the automobile had come. It would not be long till daylight. She must be getting dry. She must be getting back! Yes, here was the narrows, that big boulder, one on either side. She passed her little wet hands over them lightly and felt herself lifted and borne along in a bliss she had not know since childhood. So cool, so dark, so sweet! Just one minute more! A soft, deep cloud blew over the thready old moon. The hemlocks dipped and bowed and the shadows were deep where the ferns dripped cool, and the old Mercer bell tolled One! Two! Three! It was time to get out!

CHAPTER XVIII

EMILY DILLON's lawyer had been away for a week on a fishing-trip where he hadn't got a letter, nor seen a newspaper once, and when he came back to the city he found everyone talking about the Dillon Case, and wondering what would turn up next. Mothers kept their young daughters in after dark unless they were protected by some trusty mankind, and women avoided the upper trolley which necessitated a short walk through a lonely wood. One and all pitched upon this spot as the place where Emily Dillon had met her fate. The streams and ponds for miles around the vicinity were dragged, the woods faithfully searched where a body could possibly be hidden, and special police were sworn in to be on duty at lonely places and escort late travelers to their homes. It was a time of great excitement, but still the days went by and Emily Dillon's body was not discovered.

Cautiously, after much inquiry and investigation, Miss Dillon's lawyer set about an investigation of his own.

He went to see Harriet Granniss, who gave it as her opinion that Emily's mind was affected. She said Emily had always been queer, but had been growing steadily queerer. She liked to be by herself, and never would tell where she was going when she went out; and she offered as evidence of her peculiarity the remarks she had made about the tomatoes just before leaving home.

He called on Ariel and found her delicate face wan with anxiety, and her great eyes gray with sorrow over her friend. He was deeply impressed with her exquisiteness, and found himself wondering if the Judson Granniss who was interested in the little stone bungalow could possibly be good enough for a girl like this, the more especially as he was reported to be the son of the Granniss person whom he had just interviewed. He wondered if this girl knew she was named in Miss Dillon's will as the legatee of the little stone bungalow, but decided not to ask. He tried to find Judson Granniss, but learned at his boarding-house that he had not been seen since the morning after the discovery of Emily Dillon's disappearance.

He visited at least a dozen Dillon cousins, and found as many opinions as to what had become of Emily, but they were one in saying that she had been a woman of unsocial nature, and in declaring their intention of searching this matter out thoroughly in case Emily really proved to be dead. They also united in declaring Harriet Granniss an interloper who had no right whatever to that house she was living in, her son a lazy loafer, the Boggs girl a huzzy, and Ariel Custer a frail unknown, probably worse than them all. Never agreeing about anything in life before, they had now joined hands to fight this thing to a finish, to get hold of Emily's estate, and by hook or crook to break that will somehow and get that house back into the family. Among them all there had been not one but Ariel Custer to shed a tear for the quiet little woman who had so mysteriously dropped out of their daily life. The lawyer went back to town disgusted, and determined to keep Miss Dillon's will in the background as long as possible. It was of course not his place to bring it out until it had been proved beyond the possibility of a doubt that Emily Dillon was really dead.

The days passed and some of the cousins began to get excited. Harriet Granniss drove around in Emily's car, piloted by the Boggs girl, who was greatly in evidence, and carried her head high. Harriet must have known what they were saying about her, she was sharp enough to understand that such things would be said under the circumstances, but she believed in keeping up a good appearance, so she went to prayer-meeting as usual, and gave a large donation to the missionary society. The cousins thought such conduct was scandalous, it was time something was done and that woman turned out of the house that never had belonged to her anyway. One elderly Dillon spinster tried to have the house searched, and went so far as to suggest that perhaps Mrs. Granniss had their cousin hidden somewhere, locked up, and tortured. Such things had been. In short, they took a wider interest in Emily Dillon gone, disappeared, dead perhaps, than they had ever taken when she was alive. And always with a tidy eye to the property, for it began to appear little by little that Emily Dillon had wide holdings here and there. A little farm well rented and growing in value, some shares in a gold mine out west, a row of stores in a busy part of the city, another of small city homes always filled, a house here, and a bungalow there, and no telling where the rent had been deposited. Bolton bank might not be the only one, it was hinted. Now that the matter had come out in the papers there came letters from hospitals and homes for orphaned children telling of her quiet deeds, and expressing anxiety and a willingness to help in searching for her body. The whole vicinity seemed to be suddenly interested in the little quiet woman who was gone so mysteriously.

Jud Granniss came back with deep lines on his face and eyes that seemed not to have slept for days. He had been tramping the woods all over the county, looking in most unheard of places, but all to no avail. He found the letter from the lawyer awaiting him that had been written about the little bungalow at Miss Dillon's request. It had been missent to Glendale instead of Glenside and so had not reached him sooner. In great trouble he took it at once to Ariel Custer. Together they wept over and worried about that letter.

"It was great to her," said Jud, struggling with the huskiness of his voice, "but Ariel, I'm afraid it's going to make a lot of trouble for us—if—she—doesn't come back!"

"Why! How could it, Jud?" asked Ariel, startled.

"Don't you see? They might think we had used undue influence to make her write that letter. I think I'll go right down to that lawyer's office and explain to him that we can't afford to take the house now. We can't think of getting married anyhow till this matter is all cleared up."

"Of course!" said Ariel, decidedly. "O dear! Jud, why weren't we content just as we were until the right time came? To think how happy we were that day down by the creek and now here is all this trouble!"

"Maybe we haven't seen the worst of it yet," said Jud, with a worried look. "Ariel, don't you talk! You just go about your business and don't mention Miss Dillon. If you're asked any questions tell the truth, of course; but O Ariel! I can't get over it to think I got you into all this mess!"

"Why, there isn't any mess for us, dear," said Ariel, fluttering the palm of her little hand over the lapel of his coat in a way she had.

"Why, there's nothing except our sorrow over dear Miss Emily."

"Well, I hope so," said Jud, only half comforted, "but don't you talk and don't you worry, even if I don't come over often. Pray, Ariel, pray."

After he had kissed her good-bye and gone away in the darkness, Ariel stood a long time on the little front porch hugging to herself those last words of his. To think that he should have told her to pray instead of swearing as he used to do at a God who let this trouble come upon them! It was worth while passing through some trouble just to hear him say that and to know there was real trust behind it. Jud was being tested and was keeping his vow.

A few days later Si Hawkins and Ephraim Sears were down at Copple's Creek quite early in the morning fishing near the old swimming-hole. It was four weeks since the news had drifted to Mercer of the disappearance of Emily Dillon, and nothing had as yet been heard to give the slightest clue to what had happened to her. The two men discussed it as they sat in the hazy sunshine and fished.

"Quar," said Ephraim with a quid in the corner of his cheek. "You'd thunk they'da found her by this ef she was off her head."

"Wal, she certainly did look nutty that day, wading in the creek, her a grown woman! Pretty little feet she had, too. Ef 'twas her. You know I didn't get a good look at her face rightly 'fore you made me come away."

"It was her all right; I knowed her even when she was walkin' the bridge. You can't cheat me, an' I got a real good look in her eye when we was down behind the rushes."

It was a few minutes after that that they found the body. One of the lines caught in the clothing, and they pulled together and finally succeeded in dragging it to shore. But the body had been in the water a long time, and the face was covered by a heavy veil, tied close and sodden to the flesh.

"It's her, all right," said Ephraim Sears, in a grim old voice. "I sorta had a hunch sompin' happened to her that day. She musta been nutty! Si, you sure that was the thirteenth? The paper said she disappeared the fourteenth."

"Oh, well, papers mostly make mistakes," declared Si. "Say, we better git the coroner."

The inquest was held that night in the Mercer morgue, and all Glenside heard by wireless-heartless before nine o'clock that Emily Dillon's body had been found.

"The body was badly disfigured," reported an important old man who had kept the telephone-wires hot with curiosity, "but they identified her by her clothing and by the money which was found on her person. It was folded each bill by itself the way they say she always folded her money. There was two fives and some ones in a little pocket in her skirt. Oh, yes, there's no doubt but it was suicide. 'Cause if anybody had killed her why wouldn't they have took her money?"

Later in the day other facts leaked out, some of which appeared in the paper. Emily Dillon had left packages in one of the Bolton stores to be called for, and the girl who had called for them wore a long gray veil, and came in a car driven by a tall young man with black hair. The face of the corpse had been covered completely by a long gray veil, wound about the neck twice and firmly fastened around the left arm. The whole county began to sit up and take notice. It was whispered that the head had been badly bruised, although some declared that there had been no marks of strangulation. There was a paragraph in the paper saying that one noted doctor, present at the inquest, declared the woman had been smothered.

Excitement rose high when Emily Dillon's will was read and it was found that she had left the bulk of her property to Jud Granniss. And the little bungalow which everybody had supposed was the property of S. S. Packard had been left—of all people—to Ariel Custer!

Harriet Granniss shut her lips hard and narrowed her eyes as if she saw a new clue, and the town looked at one another aghast. Ariel Custer! H'mmmm! Why, yes, Ariel Custer went with Jud Granniss. And the Dillon house now belonged to Jud's mother! Jud and his mother were at outs! Or, were they? Wasn't that perhaps a ruse? Wasn't it perhaps—but no—why, it *couldn't* be—but of course if there were anything it would be found out— Why didn't somebody do something?

Then the paper stated that a new witness had been found who declared that Emily Dillon had been seen several days before her drowning, if drowning it was, walking alone across the old Copple's bridge near Mercer, and wading barefoot in the creek near the old farm which had been her childhood's home.

People said: "Ah! Poor thing! Then it *was* suicide!"

Later in the day the news came out that Ephraim Sears of the old Mercer farm, had heard an automobile going rapidly across the lower meadow down toward the creek at two o'clock in the morning. He had listened until it returned a few minutes later, and then had gone to sleep and forgotten it although it had seemed a queer place for a car to go in the dark night where there was no regular road. Tracks of a car turning had been found in the wet clay of the bank. Then people began to look at one another harder than ever and to whisper words.

A car! Harriet Granniss has a car! Jud Granniss drove it! Ariel! Jud! The car! A gray veil! H'mmm.

The old swimming-hole was dragged for further clue, but brought forth nothing more important than a dead dog in a bag loaded with bricks to make it sink.

The next morning it was stated that there were complications and the body was to be exhumed and a second post-mortem to take place to settle whether or not the woman had been poisoned. Excitement ran high.

They gathered together everybody who had any connection with the matter. They called in several great specialists, both of medicine and justice, and a great many unpleasant questions were asked and answered. Harriet Granniss was there with her rampant feathers, her aggressive mouth and belligerent eyes, calm and defiant. Judson Granniss was there, looking years older, with lines of care and responsibility graven about his nice strong mouth and chin, and a protective look in his eyes when he glanced at Ariel. Ariel Custer was there, her gray-green eyes wide with apprehension, and her lips set bravely to face and answer anything that might come. The Boggs girl was there, sitting insolently beside Harriet Granniss, occasionally giving an indolent chew to the gum she always kept ready. All the Dillon cousins were there with their lorgnettes and their spectacles, and their eyeglasses, and their dried-up or their pompous looks, as the case might be. And every last one of them from the least unto the greatest looked defiant askance at Harriet Granniss the interloper, Miss Boggs the upstart, Judson Granniss who dared to be son to Harriet, and Ariel the unknown. If they had been foul vermin the Dillon skirts could not have been more carefully withdrawn, or the Dillon noses held higher, and one was even heard to say, speaking of their deceased but unmourned relative, and the house he had willed away out of the family, "Poor Jacob! He wasn't himself when he did it, of course!" Through it all Harriet Granniss sat with her head held high and her Congregational-Missionary-Porch-Meeting air of virtuous endurance.

They laid the poor little bit of disfigured clay back in the tomb until the resurrection, after they had recorded all the bits of evidence that were to be found from examination, and the relatives and friends and judiciary went to their homes and shook their heads. Things looked bad for the Grannisses. It was said that the Dillons were going to protest the will. It was said they were going further back and see what they could do towards restoring the Granniss house to the Dillon family. It was whispered that evidence was being gathered and would soon be in hand, and that a murder trial might be the result.

It was then that Judson Granniss went to the lawyer and declared that he wished to renounce all right to the property that had been left to him, and that Ariel Custer also refused to accept the bungalow that had been left to her. And people said: "Oh, yes! They're getting cold feet! They ought to have thought of that before!" But Harriet Granniss held on her way and declared to her anxious son that she meant to have her rights and no Dillon was going to cheat her out of them!

It only took a week for the gossiping part of the town to fix it all up just how the murder had been committed. It was called murder plain out now, and old residents who had moved away and come back for a visit, spoke of it in lowered tones and said: "Well, what do you think of our *murder* case? Isn't that *awful*? When is the trial coming off?"

Ariel Custer wilted right down under the fire and had to be sent to the hospital. She hadn't been eating enough lately, and had stayed up nights far into the mornings trying to eke out her scanty salary and save a little to get married with, so she had no reserve force, though her spirit was exceeding strong and she still could smile wistfully at Jud and say gently: "It's somehow coming out all right, Jud. I know *He* will not fail us. We must be willing to say, 'Though He slay me, yet will I trust Him.'" Poor Jud could only press her hand and turn his head away to hide the trouble in his eyes. For Jud was deeply troubled about Ariel—her strong sweet spirit was enmeshed in such a frail young body that had already borne much sorrow and anxiety.

Judson Granniss went about these days with bowed head and worked in the mill as long as he was allowed, utterly apart from his mates. It was already as if he had borne the brand of Cain in his forehead, and he was not surprised when he was laid off. Men did not want to work side by side with a murderer suspect!

CHAPTER XIX

THE Boggs girl was still a fixture with Harriet Granniss, and drove the car around a great deal at high speed, chewing gum nonchalantly, and appearing to enjoy the notoriety. There was an insolence about her straight black bobbed hair, and the way she wore the slouchy tam on one side of her big head that precluded criticism. She showed plainly that she was being what she was because she *wanted* to be that way and *liked* to have people shocked by it. She made exceeding free with men about the town, joked a lot about the coming trial, and pretended to enjoy the prospect.

But Harriet Granniss went her grim and arrogant way unmoved. This was her house and here she stayed if heaven and earth should fall. What Emily Dillon chose to do about dying did not concern her. She was here and respectable, and she had been here and respectable all the time, and she could prove it, and she wasn't going to pay the slightest attention to any trumped-up gossip about her having connived at Emily's death with her son and that washed-out, spineless creature called Ariel that he had associated himself with. So she went to prayer-meeting regularly as ever and walked heavily home alone through the darkness, for she didn't seem to succeed in making the Boggs girl go often. But virtue was her line, and virtue should be hers to the end of time.

Then at last the slow mesh of the law in the hands of the dignified and indignant Dillons enfolded the victims, and Harriet Granniss, Judson Granniss, Ariel Custer and the Boggs girl was summoned to answer a charge of murder in the first degree. It is not likely the Boggs girl would have been included if she had not held herself in the public notice so persistently, but her skill with the car, her daredevil-eye and her impudent air were too much for the Dillons to swallow and once their venom was started there really were a lot of things that pointed toward her collusion in the matter. So the trap was set, warrants issued, and the day of the trial dawned.

Out of all the townful of Christians and heathen, not one had been found to really stand out against public opinion and befriend the four. Of course there had not been wanting a few acquaintances who had expressed regret. One had gone so far as to bring Harriet Granniss a large bunch of flaming dahlias on the morning of the trial. These she had handed promptly back to the donor with the grim remark that it wasn't her funeral yet she was thankful to say.

It was Emily Dillon's lawyer who had quietly distinguished himself by offering to take the case of the accused four. Harriet Granniss had promptly and rudely declined the offer for herself and the Boggs girl, with a covert sneer that more than hinted that his own innocence might bear looking into. How much, for instance, had he received for fixing up that ridiculous will for Ariel and Jud?

Harriet Granniss had a nasty quirk of revenge in her make-up that made it possible for her to charge her own son with connivance at a murder. Not that she really thought that anything would ever be proved against him, of course, but she wanted to punish him for going against her in the matter of the girl, and she felt sure Ariel would be proved guilty.

But Judson Granniss gratefully accepted the services of the well-known and successful lawyer for Ariel and himself. Harriet, on her part, hunted out a smart but disagreeable young man from the city to defend her case, and he, seeing her spirit, did his cunningest to throw suspicion from his own clients upon her son and the frail young girl, with a decided specializing on the girl.

So at last the stage was set and the day of the trial dawned.

CHAPTER XX

IT WAS crowded and warm in the courtroom when they entered, for the day before had been frosty, and fires had been started vigorously; but Ariel shivered as she sat down and gazed about in horror on the crowd assembled to gloat over her humiliation. She had the atmosphere of something exquisitely delicate and tender being rudely, ruthlessly crushed in barbarous hands. There were rows and rows of Glenside people, Congregationalists, Methodists, all the other denominations, and two solid rows of Dillons, male and female, importance and recrimination in the countenances. She recognized Mrs. Smalley, and two or three mothers of her Sunday School Class of boys she had recently been teaching as a substitute; also the man whose daughter she had helped in arithmetic evenings, but none of them had a friendly light of pity for her; and away back by the door she saw the brutal—handsome face of her employer watching her with a kind of gloating triumph as if now he had her where he wanted her. He had dared to send her word the night before that if she would accede to his wishes he would see that she went scot-free. His eyes sought hers now in her first wild look about the sea of curious and unfriendly faces, and his look sickened her so that she swayed in her chair and turned white. The Dillon lawyer saw it and stooped pityingly, whispering:

"Just take courage, Miss Custer. We have a good case. Don't let them see you break down. It will be bad for you and bad for Mr. Granniss also. Remember you've him to think of as well as yourself."

With a brave look Ariel answered him and set her delicate lips firmly. They should not see her fright and weakness. She would be brave and somehow help to get Jud free. She herself felt that her life was almost flickering out, but for his sake it must go out bravely and without a blemish. So she sat and faced the day and the regiment of eyes, and set herself to be strong and pray without ceasing for the strength she knew she had not in herself.

Early that morning she had found a wonderful verse, and she had sent the reference to Jud by Dick who was her faithful envoy. 1 Peter 4:12, 13. She knew he had his little pocket testament, her birthday gift to him, always in his pocket. She saw him take it out covertly and look it up. His eyes met hers. The words were going over now in her mind: "Beloved, think it not strange concerning the fiery trial which is to try you, as though some strange thing happened unto you: But rejoice, inasmuch as ye are partakers of Christ's sufferings; that, when his glory shall be revealed, ye may be glad also with exceeding joy."

Jud's eyes met hers. There was a look of understanding in them, of faith, as if he had taken hold of the message from above. Ariel felt a thrill of exultation even there in the courtroom. God had not forgotten and Jud was standing his test. And suddenly another Bible verse came to her mind:

"Fear not them which kill the body, but are not able to kill the soul—"

Strange how those wonderful words spoke themselves into her heart as if her Lord indeed stood by and spoke them in her ear, keeping His promise to be with her through the fire, and through the floods. A new strength came to her, and she sat up, brave and unafraid. Whatever came, God was theirs, and He would do what seemed good to Him. Why should they be afraid? They were His, and He had said they were of more value than many sparrows. He stood by a sparrow's dying bed. If they must die He would be there too. So why fear?

People wondered at Ariel Custer's sweet composure. It argued ill for her with the Dillon cousins. They called it brazenness. They said among themselves, "How could anyone be so brazen?" as she sat there in conscious realization of her Lord close by her side. But then how could they understand? Not many of them knew the Lord even with a speaking acquaintance.

If Emily Dillon, sweet soul, as she had sat in her little tatted nightgown in the cool of the summer night planning her sweet plans for the happiness of these two young things, could have foreseen this day and the sorrow on their suddenly aged young faces, what sorrow would have been hers! But Emily Dillon had passed beyond the vision of little Glenside and its doings, having wrought her sweet worst for the two she loved best, and they were here alone. Ariel thought of it as she looked around with a desperate feeling that somehow her old friend would be there among the rest and would rise and put her in the right. She thought of the last time she had seen her sitting in the fragrant darkness of the honeysuckle-vine, so wholesome and little in her white skirt and shirtwaist, with a bit of a ribbon-bound palm-leaf fan in her hand, gently rocking back and forth and stirring the sweetness from the vine into the soft night about them. She thought of the kind action that had left the fatal gift of the coveted bungalow, and smiled wanly to herself as she stared into the space of blurred faces, seeing them not at all. Emily Dillon had meant to do such a beautiful thing, and all these humans here judging before her had turned it into such a horrible thing. She shuddered as she thought of all her lost dreams and beautiful hopes, as she looked toward Jud with his dark head bowed and the lines so heavily marked in her dear face. They had not been able to thank their dear friend for the beauty she had meant to put into their lives, but sometime, up in heaven, perhaps very soon if this awful trial went against them, she would be able to slip to her old friend's side and whisper to her how dear she had been. It was not her fault that all this horror had come. If only she and Jud could go together! Perhaps they would! Who knew? It was awful to go in such a way, with a false reputation; but up there—up there surely everything would be set right. There was a day coming when even Dillons would see the truth, and everybody would know. "For there is nothing covered, that shall not be revealed; neither hid that shall not be known." She and Jud would not have to bear this false accusation throughout eternity. It would all be made right some day. Ariel closed her eyes and leaned her head down on her hand. The room seemed to whirl before her and she looked more like her name than ever. Someone brought her a glass of water, and she drank it and sat up again courageously determined to be brave to the end.

The day wore on and the trial proved more and more exciting as witness after witness was called and added choice bits one after another to the growing mass of evidence that seemed to be slowly shutting these four away from their kind into an outer darkness of horror.

It was late in the afternoon of the second day, and the little sneak of a Granniss lawyer had managed to make a pretty strong impression that his two clients were innocent and Jud and Ariel had been the sole plotters for the murder. He had cross-questioned Ariel, making her admit the expedition that she and Jud had made to Mercer to the vicinity of the creek. How he had found out about it only the devils of the underworld could tell perhaps but he brought it out at such an opportune time, and in such a way as to make it appear that this important fact had been purposely hidden. Before he was through there was no further question in the minds of most of his listeners but that Ariel and Jud had brought undue pressure to bear upon the deceased in influencing her to leave them both money and house, and had then plotted carefully to get her out of the way. He even hunted out like a needle in the proverbial haystack, the man and boy who got off the same car with Emily Dillon on that memorable morning. He had brought to the witness-stand the two men who had driven down the Pike and seen Ariel in her green organdie. He had primed and bribed old Ephraim Sears and Silas Hawkins, until they told a wonderful tale about the two who had rented his canoe and lingered long about the old swimming-hole and the stepping-stones; and he somehow managed to connect it inevitably with the coming of the poor lady in her bare feet to that identical spot. The courtroom was very still when Ephraim Sears got done and Silas Hawkins briefly corroborated all that he had said. Not even when the town-meeting had been swayed so much against their will in favor of keeping the school tax down, had Ephraim Sears made such an impression, and he felt immensely pleased with himself. He held on to his stub of a beard and pulled it out straight in front, as was his habit when greatly excited, and he shifted the quid in his cheek to the other side, and looked around complacently on the crowded audience. This was the moment he had waited for and he looked over at Si and nodded contentedly.

It hardly seemed necessary to the onlookers after this that Emily Dillon's lawyer should go through the form of defending the two who sat there with guilt plainly marked on their haggard countenances. But, of course, justice was justice and the law said that all criminals had a right to defense. If there was anything left that could be said let it be said quickly. They settled back with foregone conclusion written plainly in their eyes, and prepared to listen to a vain harangue.

The lawyer had risen and was addressing the judge. His clear, cultured voice was like a breath of another atmosphere, after the snarl of Harriet's defender, and caught their jaded attention. Perhaps he had something up his sleeve, after all—some new morsel that would be interesting and satisfy their morbid curiosity, even if it proved nothing.

Then, even as the lawyer turned his face toward them and opened his mouth to call his first witness there came a breath of something strange and tense into the atmosphere; no noise, just a quiet opening of the door at the back of the room; no stir, yet every eye turned to look, and every head was stretched up over his neighbor's, to see who had come in at that door, for that it was something startling and unexpected the hush and the awe in the entire room made plain to even the farthest occupant.

CHAPTER XXI

WHEN Emily Dillon had walked that portulaca-bordered path through the white pillared gateway and down the pleasant street of her home village her heart had been light and happy, and there had been a smile on her face that was good to see. She nodded cheerily to the milkman and the iceman with that little rosebud smile she always wore, and tripped away into the summer like a happy robin. The milkman and iceman had both taken off their caps respectfully as they always did and looked after her with a warm feeling of friendship. Somehow she always made them feel as if they were gentlemen when they passed her.

She chatted with the butcher for a minute or two while she waited for her car, and he remarked as he went back to his customer in the shop: "That's one good little woman, that is!"

The errand to the Bolton Bank consumed small time, and she glanced at the additional sum in her bank book with satisfaction. It wasn't a large account, but there was a reason why she wanted it to be as big as possible just now, and the sum thus added brought the account up to round numbers.

Pausing as she stepped out of the bank she happened to glance across the way to the little ice-cream parlor, and yielded to a childish desire for a plate of the delicious home-made ice-cream that was always served there. Foolish and sinful, Harriet would have called it, at that hour in the morning! But when one was free as air, and felt like eating ice-cream, why should one not do it? Besides it was hot, and ice-cream would be cooling. So she tripped across the street and ordered a dish of vanilla ice-cream and a piece of chocolate layer-cake; and while she ate she thought of Rebecca Ford and wished she could be there eating ice-cream along with her. Why had she never planned to take Rebecca for an outing somewhere? It could have been done in the city well enough without Harriet ever finding out. Having once made a break she wondered why she had never done it many more times. Well, she would send something to Rebecca, anyway.

When she had finished eating she bought a cocoanut cake and some macaroons and had them done up to be called for. Then she tripped over to the drug-store and telephoned to Rebecca Ford's daughter-in-law in Mercer to know when they were going after their mother. The woman said Tom was going that afternoon and could drive around by the way of Bolton as well as not and get the packages. Emily knew by the eager way in which she said, "Cakes? Oh, *that's* nice!" that they would not be forgotten and that a large portion of them would not be eaten by Rebecca. But then life was like that. You couldn't help it. She sighed as she went out to the corner where the Short Line passed and wished she had thought to do something like that the last day Rebecca was at the house. She could easily have slipped her something after Harriet went away.

There was a strange conductor on the car she boarded, so she rode all the way to the city instead of changing to another line a little beyond Glenside as she had intended, which proves how easily conductors can be mistaken about things they think they are sure of, and when she reached the city it was quarter to twelve. She looked at the clock on the City Hall Tower and compared it with her quaint old-fashioned watch a trifle nervously. She had a great many things to do before night and must not waste a minute. She was glad she had stopped for the ice-cream, for now she wouldn't need any lunch, and it took so much longer to get waited on in the city than out at Bolton.

She went at once to the nearest big department-store, and bought a small folding map of the United States, one that contained all the principal cities plainly marked. She retired to a quiet corner of the waiting-room and spread it out on her lap before a window with her back turned to every one else, and there she diligently perused it for twenty minutes, coming at last with her finger to a little black dot that pleased her, for a light broke out in her face.

"That's it!" she whispered, softly, to herself, with a furtive look around her, "I was sure it was that."

Folding her map in its creases carefully, and stuffing it into her handbag she flitted from her corner with definite purpose in her face and hurried across the street to another bank where she also had an account of which Harriet had no knowledge. She had found it convenient to make this arrangement on account of her small charities here and there which she did not care to discuss with her housemate. Here she drew a goodly check to her own order and asked to have her safety deposit box brought, as she wished to get something out of it. She was shown into the little waiting-room and the box put before her.

She carefully put away her money, some in her bag for immediate use, some in a tiny buttoned pocket in the bosom of her dress, and unlocking her safety deposit box took out of it a lot of Liberty Bonds which she knew were negotiable at any time. These she wrapped in a handkerchief and pinned securely into her blouse. Then she locked her box, carried it to the attendant, and went out upon the street.

There came a breathless feeling as she stood again on the sidewalk with the hurrying city life all about her. She had just taken a great and decisive step. It was not too late to step back and undo it. She felt almost bewildered, but very happy, and strangely light again as she had done the day before when she ran away and went wading in the creek. She felt as if she wanted to do something terribly frivolous, and the first thing that stared her in the face was a hair-dresser's sign.

Emily Dillon had always wanted to have her hair shampooed and dressed in a professional way, but it was a wish that had never before dared come to the surface. In her father's time she would never have done such a thing. He would have guyed her to the end of her days and ragged her about the foolish waste of money. And then along came Harriet, and she would have been worse. Harriet held that a woman who had her hair washed by someone else was a lazy huzzy and that was all there was about it. Emily never felt that it was worth while to give Harriet any additional themes for remarks. So she had patiently scrubbed her own soft hair in the wash-bowl through the years. But now, a sudden impulse seized her. Why should she not do as she pleased? She was free. No one to hinder—no one to know! She looked breathlessly about to be sure no Glenside shoppers were coming in either direction, and then she hopped across the street with her bird-like motion and disappeared into the stairway that led to the hair-dressing parlors.

"I should like my hair washed, and done up some new way," she announced, serenely in a sweet voice that one would never take for the first time in a place like this. "Have you time for me?"

"If you'll take it right now," said the girl with the henna permanent wave, looking at the clock speculatively, just as if it were an everyday affair for Emily Dillon.

Emily slipped into the curtained booth indicated and took off her hat with a wildly beating heart. Her hand was trembling so that she could hardly get hold of her jet hatpin, but she was smiling as she sat down in front of the big mirror, and she felt that she was off, just as she had felt the first time Nate Barrett put her on his big bobsled and took her down the hill.

An hour later a new Emily Dillon came down the steps to the street. Her hair was waved becomingly and made a soft frame for her face. Her eyes had lost their tired look. She had rested with them shut while her hair was being done and thought out a great many lovely plans. Things had been vague in her mind before, but now they became quite definite. When she caught a glimpse of herself in the mirror as she was getting into the elevator it almost took her breath away, and her new self with her hair done like other people seemed to give her confidence.

Her first move was to go to the railroad station and consult the information-desk. She came away in half an hour with a timetable, a ticket, and a sleeper-reservation all neatly sealed in a railroad envelope and tucked away in her handbag; for Emily Dillon was about to run away!

But first, she felt she must have a new hat.

The old black toque did not fit at all with her hair that way. It had been with difficulty that she forced it on at all. So she made her way to a milliner's and emerged a little while later with a love of a gray hat wreathed about with gray ostrich-feathers. She scarcely dared look at herself in the store windows as she passed. She knew that was no hat for her father's daughter to buy, no hat for a sensible, mature Dillon to wear. Harriet would have disapproved it with a fervor that almost made her shrink and falter and turn back, for Harriet always said that ostrich-feathers were extravagant because they were "so very, *very* perishable!"

But to Emily they filled a long desire, and it thrilled her unspeakably with a soft little joy as she walked along and felt the feathers floating with her. When she caught a glimpse of herself in a passing mirror she caught her breath with wonder. She had never supposed she could look like that. She was not vain, only surprised and pleased. If it had been another woman she was looking at she would have said: "Why, she's almost *pretty!*" But Emily never would harbor such a thought about herself. She just felt pleased and comfortable.

Down to the woman's coat-and-suit department she hurried, for a hat like that merited a different dress. She bought a coat and skirt of soft dark-blue taffeta that wouldn't crush. It had little huddled pools of fine braiding here and there, and some floating braided panels on the skirt that gave her more than ever the look of a bird with its wings held tidily close.

The hem had to be taken up and a little change made in the coat, so while she waited for her second fitting she went and bought two sheer white blouses, delicate with embroidery and fine lace, and a dark-blue georgette blouse, trimly tailored with pipings of gray charmeuse.

It was while she was adjusting this blouse in the dressing-room after the second fitting, and the saleslady had gone to have her old dress wrapped that Emily realized her shoes were not up to the rest of her toilet. Her heart beat high until a little wild rose bloomed in either cheek. Was there anything out of the way in a woman of her years wearing *gray suede shoes* if she chose? Yes and *silk stockings* to match? Other women of good repute did it, and why shouldn't she wear beautiful things on this one trip of her life? She had saved and stayed in the background all her life. Not that she cared to come to the front now even, but she did want just once to see how it would seem to be dressed in some of the pretty things that were floating so freely around the world. Why hadn't she thought of it before? Gray shoes cost no more than black, at least than some black ones, and anyway, she had money enough to indulge a desire for beauty now and then.

"They're very comfortable, too, and durable," said the

salesman as he finished fitting them on a few minutes later, and Emily, almost at the verge of tears trembled out a bit of a smile and said: "Well, I'll take them."

At ten minutes to six she stepped forth from the door of a big department-store, gray as to hat, shoes, gloves and veil, in her trim new suit and bearing in her hand a pretty new traveling-bag of handsome leather, fitted with brushes and other toilet-articles. It was filled with a dainty selection of fine undergarments, a feather-weight silk raincoat, and a soft little one-piece frock of silky, cobwebby gray that looked like the underside of a gray dove's wing when it unfurls, and had a round neck and frilly lace in the sleeves. She was almost afraid to think about it as she stepped off in her dark-gray suede oxfords, and wondered if anybody from Glenside would know her if they met her. She hurried out of sight into a side street to an inviting tea-room where she took refuge in a high-backed seat by a pink-shaded candle-lighted table and ordered chicken à la King, fruit salad and cherry pie à la mode. She hadn't an idea what any of them were, written down in that way, for she was not a frequenter of restaurants, but she felt that something was due her new self tonight and she was too excited to do anything in the old well-tried way. She ate her supper joyously, and gradually calmed down enough to think over her purchases. They had not been so very expensive. The suit was out of a sale, the gray frock a little French model put down because there were no more; "a sample" they called it. The raincoat was a great bargain, cheaper than the usual plain black ones, and the shoes were the last of the summer sale, a wonderful thing for the money, on account of her having such a small foot and being able to wear an odd size. There had been nothing in the whole lot that she did not have to have unless perhaps she ought to have been willing to wear her old black suit. But she looked down at the neatly wrapped bundle beside her new bag with a degree of triumph. That was one thing she would not do, she would not wear that black suit on her expedition. When she came to think it over the only crime she had committed against her traditional conscience had been to buy giddy colors, and after all gray and dark blue were not so *very* gay. Harriet wore dark blue, and flowered things even, and Harriet was two years her senior. Why should she be condemned to black? But when she came to think of it, black, black, black had been her garb for the last twenty years. Black for her mother, her aunt, her grandmother, and then for her father. And because of the hateful way in which the cousins had treated her father she had worn the black with only the change of a white blouse now and then all these four long years. And it was time and right she should have a change.

She finished her supper and picked up her things, fitting on the new gloves with a pleasant thrill, and decided to get rid of that black dress. She had bought a new dark blue silk umbrella with a silver handle, and with that and her new bag she had plenty to carry without the package. She came out into the street again and walked along wondering wht she could do with it. She didn't exactly like to send it to Rebecca Ford, that would perhaps cause comment and excite questions. There must be some poor body that would be glad of it. Then she looked up and saw coming down the street slowly with a weary gait a sorrel horse and an old wagon with the charmed legend "SALVATION ARMY" in faded letters on its side. The wagon was full of old chairs and piles of newspapers, and Emily stepped quickly to the curb and signaled the driver, a scraggly old man, who drew up his horse abruptly and looked at her.

"Won't you just put this package in your wagon?" she said. "It's some clothing that I want to give away. It will be perfectly good for somebody that's in need."

"Oh, sure, lady, sure. Thank you, lady!" the man said, reaching out with alacrity, and in a moment more he was driving briskly away toward Market Street, and Emily with cheeks rosy from her deed was walking as briskly in the direction of the station.

She checked her bag and umbrella and then went out to amuse herself until train-time, which was close on to midnight.

CHAPTER XXII

A COOL breeze had risen, and the oppression of the day was gone. She stepped out into the street with a lightness and finality as if she were stepping into a new life. Nothing had done her as much good as giving that old black serge to the Salvation Army. Not that she had anything against the serge. It was neat and well made and fitted her, but it seemed somehow to be a sort of symbol of her old life of time-serving, and she enjoyed the thought that she had nothing now but these new beautiful things, and she wouldn't have to save them, because she hadn't anything else to wear. Oh, doubtless she would buy some plain things to wear everyday when she got somewhere, but now her life called for new and beautiful things, for she was going to be a new creature. She walked down a wide, pleasant street without particularly noticing where she was going. The city was not an old story to her, because she had not gone to it as often as some people do, and everything she saw was of interest. She came to a great stone church, with its door wide open and people going in. It was a Methodist church and it must be prayer-meeting night, so she went in too, and sat for an hour in the sweet, quiet atmosphere and bowed her head in thanksgiving. She was having a good time and she wanted to be grateful for it. Whatever came of her expedition she was enjoying it now, and she sang the closing hymn, "Abide with me," with a sweet, birdlike soprano that had never been overstrained by too much joy, and tripped shyly out ahead of everybody into the lighted streets. Next she went to a moving-picture show, and cried and laughed over a sweet story of childhood to which her guardian angel must have surely directed her faltering gray-suede footsteps.

It was eleven o'clock when that was over and she felt almost frightened to be in the streets alone so late at night, the *city* streets, and all dressed up this way. But she saw there were throngs of nice people and plenty of women alone like herself, and she suddenly discovered that her dress was in no way noticeable, which made her feel much better. She wended her way back to the station, unchecked her bag and umbrella, bought a magazine and a cake of chocolate, and went shyly out to her first journey in a sleeping-coach.

The porter made up her berth at once and she crept into it awkwardly, glad that no one seemed to be watching her, and drew the curtains close just as the train was starting. But she did not set about making herself ready for sleep at once. She put her hat in the paper bag the porter had brought for its protection, she slipped off her silk coat and skirt and folded them out of her way, and put her gray shoes in the little hammock that hung across the windows. Then she opened up the shade, curled herself close to the glass and looked out. The lights of the city flashed into her face sharply for a few minutes, and began to alternate with stretches of dark windows. Presently they were making their rapid course out through the suburbs. Off there to the left was Lovedale, and Glenside would be that farther group of scattered lights. The midnight train would just about now be coming in and would Harriet wait up and expect her home? Ought she to have made some explanation? But somehow—somehow—she *couldn't*. Not yet. Perhaps— But what did it matter? Harriet would not be disturbed. She was her own mistress and had a right to go wherever she liked. No one cared a whit, and Harriet would soon get used to it. Anyhow, she could always write if she thought it necessary later. Meanwhile this was an experiment, and she couldn't have made it if Harriet had had to pry into every why and wherefore. She looked off to the little patch of light in the sky that meant the street-lights of Glenside, and sighed happily to feel herself going on by. Tonight she would not sit in the little tatted nightgown and watch the wild rabbit on the lawn in the moonlight. Tonight she was out with the moon going along.

The train shot through a tunnel and rushed out past a big town, on into the woods, around a curve, and so coming reached the high trestle over Copple's Creek. Emily sat holding her breath and watching, straining her eyes in the moonlight—such a faint little thread of a moon it was really only starlight—to see the old familiar spot. Not often had she gone through Mercer on the train, for the railroad had not touched it in the old days when her father's farm on the creek was her home; but as she looked down from the high bridge she could trace the landmarks one by one; the winding glint of the water below; that first turn was where the rocks jutted out and the hemlocks swept over, and the next turn was marked by the willows! On below were the stepping-stones and the swimming-hole! And out in the broad, treeless stretch was the old farm with its low-lying roofs, its dark windows, and no sign of life. Farther on lay the little town. How its main street whirled by in the night, with only a white streak where the church-spire rose among the trees, and a blare of light where the court-house made a break in the foliage. And then it was gone!

Emily Dillon folded her new silks neatly, put the hat in a safe place where it would not be shaken away nor jammed by the motion of the train, sought out her blue-muslin kimono and wrapped herself in its new folds to lie down for pleasant slumber. But with her head on the pillow she found it a long time before she could tear her thoughts from the day and all its experiences, and in this strange, noisy rocking-cradle-bed give up her soul to sleep. She had shut the door behind her and gone out. She would not open the door into the morrow for she dared not, and so her soul beat its gray wings against the bars and fluttered long before it went to sleep.

She spent three days in Chicago.

She bought a serviceable wardrobe-trunk and filled it with a lot of pretty and suitable clothes, and a few other things that she had always wanted, but she bought nothing black. Nothing at all black, not even a book. It seemed so happy to her that she might purchase only glad colors, and she fairly revelled in the delight of looking over pretty things. She did not blossom into gaudy tastes, however, but stuck to soft pastel shades, heliotrope, pale blue, a delicate pink, and gray, so often gray or creamy white. Nothing loud or extreme, just suitable and serviceable for a quiet little woman. That was all she wanted. The only thing that troubled her was that she was doing the whole thing in a sort of underhanded way. She would rather have done it frankly, but that would have been so impossible with Harriet, and Harriet would have never let her go alone. She would have managed somehow to go along, and that of course, would have spoiled the whole thing. She never would have gone at all under those circumstances. Oh, it never *could* have been done with Harriet. But still she was so happy that she scarcely ever thought of this at all.

She took a taxi and did the city of Chicago like any sightseer, bought a book and found all the spots of interest, and then bought another ticket and went on her way. About the time the whistle in Glenside blew to call the men together to search for her, Emily Dillon was on her way to the station to take another train to bear her further away. Dear soul! And if she took thought about them at all it was to rejoice that she had made provision richly for the only two she cared a flip about in the whole Glenside village. How astonished she would have been could she have known what a stir she was making in her little old home town. I'm not sure but she would have cried and rushed right back to embrace them all if she could have looked down from her high, far journey and seen those stalwart men from the fire house, and those older men from the golf links, and the boys from the high school—and Jud! If she could have seen *Jud* with straining, bloodshot eyes, wild, disordered hair, and torn garments, plunging through the brakes and undergrowth in the deep, tangled heart of the woods, peering under great logs, over precipices, she would have trembled for the terror she had wrought in the hearts of those she had not thought bore any love for her. But oh, how her laugh would have rung out for the mercenary cousins who were so concerned for her that they were already wrangling about breaking her will! and for the poor fat partner of her house who had half killed herself putting up superfluous tomatoes, and hustling her supper up the stairs for a dramatic ending to a perfect day of revenge! But Emily Dillon never dreamed of any such thing and went on her way serenely.

She stopped to see some wonders by the way, springs, rocks, geysers, mountains, and took everything that came with that same sweet zest, but only on the side as it were, for her eyes were ever onward. And so, at last, after many days of enjoyment she came to the city of her goal.

CHAPTER XXIII

IT WAS broad bright morning in Boise City and Emily Dillon had gone to her hotel. She had made herself fresh and eaten breakfast before she ventured to let herself hunt up a telephone-book. She told herself that of course his name might not be there. He might not have a telephone. Perhaps ranchmen had no need for a telephone. Perhaps he couldn't afford one. But no, they had said he was rich. Still, Becky might have been mistaken. She kept her finger quite steady as it went down the line of B's—Bab, Bac, Bad, Bae. How many queer names there were! She found her finger going slower. She was afraid to go rapidly or come on it too soon for fear after all it might not be there at all. And she came suddenly upon it—Nathan Barrett—standing out from the page and fairly shouting to her, so that her cheeks all alone in the room by herself flamed up to coral red.

She swallowed hard a good many times, and got a drink of water before she could summon her voice to speak over the telephone.

When at last she mustered courage to call the number the answer came so promptly that it took her breath away and all power of speech:

"Hello! Barrett at the phone!" Over the years the voice came booming at her, storming the citadel of her heart, fairly trampling down all the sweet wall of patience and abnegation she had built up for her courage. Her heart took a tumble and up again to her throat, threatening to smother her. She opened her lips to speak but no sound came forth. She was weak with excitement and wonder. He was *here*, after all the years! It was *really he*, and she had *found him*. Without any trouble she had come right to him! He had been here a long time and she might have found him sooner—if she had only known! "Hello!" came the voice insistently, inquiringly, again. "This is Nathan Barrett. Who is speaking, please?"

There was something about the voice now that quieted her perturbation and she was able to articulate.

"Nathan," she said, hardly above a whisper in a little husky tone, "is that really you?"

"What? What was that? I can't hear you! Please say that again!"

Emily Dillon, frightened now at what she had said, glad that he had not heard, summoned all her studied calm, summoned to her mind the phrases she had been rehearsing all the way across the continent, and lifting up her voice in a sweet, conventional lilt such as would have been recognized at home, broke forth again:

"This is Emily Dillon, Nate—" She had tried to say "Mr. Barrett," but the words would not be spoken. "I'm taking a trip and have just heard that you live out this way. I thought I would call you up. I—you—That is, I thought it would be pleasant to hear your voice—and—perhaps you might care to call at my hotel."

"Emily! *Emily Dillon!*" There was unquestionable joy in the first utterance of her name, but a trifle of reservation in the second, although spoken even more eagerly, "Is it really you, Em'ly?" She was so glad that he had

used her own words, the words he had not heard—
"And after I've waited— Ah, after all these years! But
where— Are you alone, Em'ly?"

"Yes, I'm all alone," said Emily, eagerly. "I—I'm just
taking a little trip, you know." Her cheeks grew rosy and
it suddenly seemed audacious in her to be even taking a
trip alone. Would he think her forward, to have called
him up? "Father died about four years ago, you know,"
she finished, in explanation.

"No, I hadn't heard. Why—Em'ly! Why didn't you let
me know at once? Why didn't you write me? I'd have
come on— You know I told you—"

"But, Nate, how could I let you know when I didn't
know where you were? I didn't even know if you were
living. You had been gone so many years and no word
whatever, not even a sign. It was only a few days ago
that I heard you were living out here somewhere. I
wasn't even sure it was so, or that I would be able to
find where you were—"

"But Emily! I *wrote*. I sent you my address as soon as
I started out here, and every once in a while I sent you
a paper with something in it about my ranch, and always I put the address in the corner somewhere. And
for a long time I sent you a card on your birthday. I
thought sure your father couldn't object to that. But
when I got no answer ever I stopped, thinking it might
only rile him up and make you trouble!"

Emily Dillon's face was sad but not surprised.

"Nate! I *never got any of them*," she said earnestly.
"I'd have found a way somehow to let you know, if I
had."

There was silence for a brief instant, a silence of
growing indignation that both felt but neither voiced,
then Nathan Barrett, clear, controlled, rising to the occasion:

"Well, it's queer whatever became—but that's neither
here nor there. You're here now! You're sure there wasn't
any other reason, Emily? You didn't find someone else?
You're not married, Emily—nor going to be?"

Her sweet, childlike laugh rang out merrily now.

"Oh, no, Nate, nothing like that. There never was."

Her voice dropped shyly, then in more serious second thought: "Are you, Nate? I heard—but it might have been a mistake, of course. People get things twisted. I just called up as an old friend, you know."

She was trying to be conventional, making the best of her way out of her maze of embarrassment, but he interrupted her with a thundering note.

"Em'ly! Where are you? Which hotel? Well, stay right where you are until I get there. I'm coming this *minute*. It won't take my car long to get there."

The receiver clicked and Emily Dillon, dazed and happy, her heart thumping and her cheeks rosy, hung up her receiver. But almost immediately the bell rang again.

"Give me that number again, Central!" It was his voice. "That you, Em'ly? Em'ly, you *wait*, won't you? You *won't* go anywhere, *will* you?"

"Why, of course I'll wait," chirped Emily, joyously. "Why, that's what I came all the way out here for," she caroled, and then suddenly realized what she had said, and stopped short in horror.

"You darling!" breathed reassuringly over the phone. "Now wait. I'll be right along. But you mustn't expect the same limber youth you knew, Em'ly. I've worked right hard and there's been a good many years. I tried to keep young for you, but it was a long time to wait."

"I'm pretty old, myself, Nate. You must expect an old lady, you know," she said, sweetly. "I meant to say that at first, but I got so flustered."

"Gosh! You'll always be young to me, no matter how many years go by," boomed the hearty voice. "The years can't take away my little yella-haired, blue-eyed girl. You can say what you like, but I shan't believe it. You'll be *just the same* to me. Now Em'ly, I'm coming, and *don't you stir until I get there!*"

She hung her receiver up again and went and looked at herself in the glass, a sober sadness dropping over her gladness like a veil. That's true, he would be disappointed. She had not realized that part before. She had visualized him as fat, perhaps, and with gray hair and maybe a beard—she hoped not a beard. She liked better the thought of his firm, pleasant lips and smooth-shaven chin, but whatever he was she didn't care, for his spirit would be the same Nate. But she had not realized before that he was expecting her to be the same. She studied the little lines about her eyes, the soft looseness of the flesh about her cheeks and chin, the silver edges of her hair. She tried to remember how she had looked when she was twenty, and felt the contrast striking her soul like a death knell. All the fine dresses and hats and newly arranged hair could not bring back her youth, the pink of her cheeks like a young bud—the gold of her hair and the smoothness of her skin. Well, perhaps she had been a fool, but at least she was to see him soon. He might be disappointed in her, but she would *see* him and *hear* his voice. She would look in his eyes and know just how things had gone with him. If he was disappointed, she would know, and she could go back—or go on somewhere else, but she would be able to live her life out if she might see him once more and hear his voice.

She studied herself in the mirror critically, until the smile came back to her lips, her eyes grew full of dream visions of the old days, and she forgot her fine little wrinkles, her withered-rose complexion and the silver edges of her hair. After all, there was the same look in her eyes for him.

She had meant to wear her blue silk to meet him, but now in a sudden panic she lifted out the little gray frock from her bag where it had traveled all the way lest she might need a change for some reason. It was exquisite with a touch of embroidery and a wisp of real lace. She had scarcely fastened the heavy rope of silk that girdled it, and clasped the pearl pin that had been her mother's in the speck of fine lace that glimpsed above the round neck before there came a knock at her door. Stepping to the door quite surprised and a bit flustered that he should have arrived so soon, she met a great box in the hands of a hall-boy.

Silently, with shining eyes she carried it in and opened it, for it bore her name in unmistakable writing on the top.

Roses! Wonderful roses, a kind that she seemed never

to have seen before, long-stemmed, heavy-headed, magnificent; pale-pink, with a hint of sunset in their curved-back petals, great buds that held their heavy heads like full blossoms, yet kept their baby texture and close-folded curves like loose silk in careless grace.

She rallied by and by from contemplation of their loveliness and rang for a vase or jar to house them. She chose one gracious bud and nestled it in the lace on the front of her gown, and then she sat down before her roses and watched them. He had stopped to telephone to a florist for them before he left his house! How wonderful of him to think of a thing like that! It was almost like being a girl again to have a great sheaf of roses like that flung at her out of a strange land!

She did not have time to think all the great thoughts that flocked to her heart before another knock came to the door, and this time he stood there himself behind the boy, who had brought him up to her sitting-room. With sudden fright clutching at her heart she rose! In her little gray dress, and her little gray shoes, the rose in the frothy lace at her breast, she came forward to meet him, a little gray dove with a wondering light in her eyes.

It did not take him long to get the hall-boy out of the way, and shut the door. There he stood for an instant taking her all in. Then he came forward with both hands out.

"Emily!" he said; "Emily!" and he folded her close in his big strong arms. He waited on no ceremony, he asked no questions, he just *took* her. She was *his*. He had waited long, and now she had come, and he took her.

Emily Dillon, with a gasp of delight, laid her fine little old roseleaf face on the rough gray tweed of his coat and let him crush her there, and loved it! Old and patient and sweet, but come at last to its own.

He let her go at last and held her out at arm's length, looking her over from gray feet to silver edges of old-gold hair, but lingering longest at her eyes, those eyes with the young dreams still alive.

"You're all right, Em'ly," he said, lapsing into his boyhood's accents. "You're just perfect! I didn't know you could stay so beautiful! All these years! I wouldn't have you changed a lash. Not a lash! But Em'ly, I'm grown a rough old hulk since you saw me. Are you sure you're not sorry you came?" Emily Dillon gave one sweeping glance at the stalwart frame, the smooth, clear-cut forceful face, and the kind young eyes, and nestled close again to the gray-tweed coat, half closing her eyes and letting the widespread palm of her speck of a hand wander contentedly up and down the buttons on the front. And he, looking down, caught her lifted glance and answered it with a close pressure of his big arm, that filled her with delight.

"And there! I almost forgot!" he said, boyishly, tucking her under one arm, and fumbling with the other hand in his vest-pocket.

He pulled it out at last, a small platinum circlet with a flashing stone and drew her hand in his.

"I hope it fits," he said eagerly, as he clumsily searched for the right finger. "I told him the smallest size he had. I remembered your little, *little* hand, Em'ly! No one else ever had such a little hand!"

She lifted her head, startled, and looked at her hand as if it were a stranger, and the big, clear diamond winked back a reassurance. Not since she had started on her timorous journey had she felt until now, how right she had been to come, and she lifted gladful eyes to his, half questioningly.

"I thought we'd better go out right away and get a license and get married, don't you think so, too? Then we could go right home and get caught up in our acquaintance and decide where we'll spend our honeymoon."

She caught her breath at his precipitous plans, but he smiled a reassurance and drew her down beside him on the couch.

"I figured it all out on my way down," he said gently. "It'll save a lot of tiresome waiting, and I must say I can't wait any longer. We can go right from the courthouse to the church. There's a good Methodist church here, and a dandy little minister that knows his job. I joined the Methodist church soon as I came out here. It seemed sort o' to bring me nearer to you, you know. I can just phone him and he'll be on the job, and we can go over to the church and get the ceremony out of the way. Then we'll get a good dinner and drive home by moonlight. How does that suit you? But of course if you have other plans I don't want to be arbitrary. What had you thought about?"

Emily Dillon's cheeks grew petal-pink, and she looked up with a soft mischief in her eyes:

"Why, Nate," she said, softly, "you never asked me yet to marry you. How could I make plans?"

He held her off delightedly and watched the pink in her cheek.

"Is that so?" he asked, amusedly. "Well, now, I guess that's true. That was quite an omission on my part, wasn't it? Well, I guess we can dispense with that formality now, can't we? We've somehow got far and away beyond that, dear heart!" and he drew her close to his heart again.

So Emily Dillon put on her gray-feathered hat and her little gray veil with a gray-ribbon edge that girdled her throat and made her look like a dove again, fitted on her long gray gloves, gathered up a wisp of a long gray-silk coat she had acquired in Chicago, and went out to get married.

CHAPTER XXIV

IN THE quiet of the evening they drove home across the hills, with the stars looking down upon them, the same stars that reflected in the Copple Creek at Mercer, and a little thread of a moon rising and riding the wide sky like a tipsy boat.

"Do you realize, Emily, that we really belong to each

other at last?" said Nate, as his big hand stole from the steering-wheel and gathered hers close.

"We've always belonged, Nate," she said, simply, "and we always would even if we'd never seen each other in this world again. I knew you'd be waiting to take me into heaven, or else I'd have to wait for you by the gate."

Into the great ranch-house he ushered her, rough and made of logs, but full of conveniences and odd luxurious corners. A wide hearth of field-stone on one side, with windows on either hand, a fireplace big enough to stand in, and deep cushiony couches either side covered with Indian blankets in many designs and barbaric colors, and piled with pillows of Indian work.

On the floor were Navajo rugs and great skins of wild animals, bear, leopard, and wolf, in rich profusion. The furniture, what there was of it, was in curious harmony with the surroundings. A few chairs, a chest, and a big table of heavy, dark, carved oak as fine of line and weathered of hue as if they had come from some ancient castle hall. The ceiling was high, reaching to the roof which was faced with logs, and lighted with a sky-light that gave a curious effect of out-of-doors in the great deep room, as if one had found shelter in a quiet nook among the trees of a forest. There were electric lights everywhere, but disguised, giving the effect of sunshine and daytime. Around three sides a gallery ran, rustic in its architecture, to which a broad, low stair ascended, and from it doors were open into rooms beyond.

He lifted her out and carried her in like a little child, striding across to the couch and dropping her down while he touched a match to the fire that was laid, for the evening had grown cool; and then he turned and knelt by her side.

"My little wife," he said, tenderly. "Emily—my *wife*—welcome *home!* I tried to make it look like the woods and the places where we used to love to be. It's crude, but you shall change it as much as you like. And if it gets lonesome here for you, we'll travel or we'll move to New York, or somewhere, or even back to Glenside; just whatever you want, goes. I'm well enough off now to take care of you."

"Oh, no!" cried Emily. "No, no, no! I want to stay right here. I love it. I don't ever need to go back. I've fixed it all so I needn't. No one will be wanting me, unless it's poor Rebecca, and maybe we could send for her to come sometime."

"Rebecca! why, *Rebecca!* Sure we'll send for Rebecca! good old Rebecca, how she used to help us out of pickles! That'll be the very thing, then you won't be lonesome when I have to be away for a few hours."

And so they talked and planned their happy life.

"But first we're going to have a regular honeymoon," said Nathan, sitting down beside her on the couch and gathering her close in his arms.

And there in the firelight they planned their trip. They would do California. They would start as soon as Nathan could put his affairs in order to leave, and before the good-hearted neighbors should take it into their heads to disturb the first quiet and peace together by coming down upon them with true western welcome. They wanted each other first alone, that they might forget the years of desolation that had been between them. So, three days later, with the little new wardrobe-trunk of trousseau strapped on behind, they got into their car and rode away into the west.

The story of that trip would be too long to tell. There was not a mar nor disappointment to spoil it, and indeed it would have been hard for any such thing to have penetrated their absorbed consciousness, so long as they had each other. Emily enjoyed every minute of the wonders and looked at each marvel with keen relish, whether snow-capped summit, towering forest of the centuries, or crumbling mission building that figured in history. She drank them all in, as one enjoys each course at a banquet, yet reserves his highest interest for the guest of honor. So Emily looked to the face of her husband for her real joy. And when, after weeks had passed, they drove up again to their own ranch house and she went in and sat by the great fire that one of

Nate's servitors had prepared for them, she sank back on the cushions, looking perfectly happy and said:

"Oh, I am glad to be here!"

It was as if they had been out to purchase some pictures for their memory hall, and now were come home to the real delights.

It was after the supper had been cleared away and they had come back from the kitchen, where they had prepared and eaten their meal together, that Nate stepped over to the table and began to look over a pile of mail that he had brought from the post-office. One of the letters bore the Glenside postmark. With a quick, apprehensive glance toward his wife as if to make sure she was his, he tore it open. It was from Ike Bowman, the old friend who had recently been out to visit him, and it read:

"Dear Nate.—I thought I would write you a short note and let you know I am well, and all the family; and also to tell you the news. We haven't had anything so kind of exciting in Glenside for years, not since Bob Hooker hung himself in his father's attic because his father wouldn't let him go to South America. I guess, as you know the parties concerned, you will be glad to hear about it.

"You remember Jake Dillon, Nate? Well, you know he had a daughter. I guess you used to like Emily pretty well yourself, at least folks say you did, but then they've been talking a lot these last few weeks and you can't tell. But anyhow Emily Dillon's dead—murdered, most folks say, although it ain't proved yet; but everything is pointing that way now, and I hope the assassin, or assassins, which is more likely, will soon be brought to justice.

"She disappeared way back in August, and nobody didn't know anything about it for several days which made it hard hunting. There was a great deal of talk, and they combed the county for signs, but they never found the body for most three weeks after, and then the face was beyond identification, but they knowed her by her clothes, and by the bills she had folded up the way she used to in her pocket, each one separate by itself. But there was a lot of queer things about it and a new will was discovered, leaving the property of which there was considerable, to the folks she had been living with, and a girl the son went with. They have got evidence, and now they have arrested three persons, Mrs. Harriet Granniss the woman she lived with, who had some kind of hold on Jake Dillon, for he left the house half to her and half to Emily, all to go to her at Emily's death, if so be she died first, so you see it looks bad. Then they've arrested her son, Judson, and the girl he is so thick with, Ariel Custer, by name. They found a will leaving most of the rest of the property to those two, and there is evidence to show they drove in a car to the old Copple Creek at Mercer once or twice before her body was found there in the old swimming-hole, where we boys used to go a-swimming. They found tracks of the car, and they've got a lot more evidence up their sleeves they ain't telling, and I guess it'll go hard with them all three. Ariel Custer is a little washed-out girl who has roped in Jud Granniss and knows more about this murder than she will tell, everybody thinks. She's a stranger hereabouts, and she seems to have played her cards well, but I guess she'll get her comeuppance pretty quick. The trial comes off next month, and they really haven't any show at all, folks say. I thought you'd be interested to know of the sad end of your old friend, and I hope this finds you well and happy. Respects of the wife to you, and we'll be glad to have you stop and see us when you come this way east ever.

Your old pal,
"Ike Bowman."

Watching the look on her husband's face, Emily had stolen close to his side and was reading the letter with him. When they had finished she looked up with terror in her eyes, which were brimming with tears.

"But they can't hurt Ariel and Jud, can they?" she asked, tremblingly. "To think I thought I had fixed everything to make them happy, and give them and Harriet each a home where they could do as they pleased, and now it has turned out like this!"

She dropped in dismay upon the couch, and Nate's arms went comfortingly around her.

"Well, you certainly did kick up a fine mess when you slipped off to get married, didn't you, little wife? But there's just one thing you forgot, and its somewhere in the Bible, too, I think. It's this, 'No man liveth to himself and no man dieth to himself.' You can't even die in this world without giving account of yourself, much less get married. But now suppose you go to work and tell me everything about this. We've been so everlastingly bound up in ourselves this trip, we haven't been noticing the world at large any. Just tell me all the circumstances about the property, and the will, and your going away."

So Emily Dillon began at the beginning and told all. As the story went on, her husband looked at the date on his letter, glanced at his watch, and when she was done, said:

"Em'ly, child, do you think you could stand it to start right out again tonight? It looks to me like we're due in Glenside about now to straighten out a bad mess. This letter was written three weeks ago, and that trial's coming on any time now. Of course we could telegraph and stop the whole show, but it looks to me like there's been some real down dirty work going on, to get those two young things mixed up in a murder this way. I think the quicker we get there the quicker we can investigate the matter. Besides, I have a hunch I'd like to show Glenside my wife! What say? Shall we take the midnight train? Can you get ready? We ought to start in fifteen minutes."

Emily fluttered to her feet, her face bright with eagerness.

"Of course Nathan; I'm ready now."

She began to put on her hat and gloves, and stuff a few things back in her handbag.

Nathan called the man who had cared for the house in their absence, gave him a few directions, got out the car, and ten minutes later they were speeding over the road in the night with the little new trunk and its pretty trousseau strapped on behind, in plenty of time for the midnight train to Denver.

CHAPTER XXV

THERE was just one man in the courtroom who had not noticed the hush, nor the opening door, and that was a peppery little red-faced, red-haired lawyer for the Dillon cousins who had made it a point to object to everything possible all the way through, and just at this point, taking advantage of the momentary lull, he broke off from an intensive consultation with a Dillon cousin and sprang to his feet shouting:

"Your Honor, I object to the way my opponent is carrying this thing on. Emily Dillon is *dead!* It has been conclusively proved that she met death in a *violent way!*"

But at that instant, even while his clamorous words were bounding about and echoing against the scarred old courtroom walls, like rubber balls set a-going that could not stop, he became suddenly aware of the hush, and looked around with a bewildered air like a dog in the act of dashing against a victim who suddenly finds pepper in his eyes. He looked around to the room full of heads turned toward the open door, and there, quite quietly down the aisle in her soft gray coat, her feathered gray hat and veil, her long gray gloves and her little gray shoes, with the rose in her cheeks, a rose on her breast, and a wonderful light in her eyes, tripped Emily Dillon herself; coming straight through the astounded throng up to the front, before the judge. Behind her walked a tall handsome stranger, as if he had a perfect right to be there and protect her.

The little objecting lawyer winked and blinked behind his thick near-sighted glasses. The Dillons stretched their offended necks and looked at one another meaningfully, as much as to say that a daughter of Jake Dillon might have been expected to do some such indecent thing as coming back to life again after she had been twice buried. Harriet Granniss sat grimly offended, a lifelong grievance in her eyes, her mind on that dramatic supper under her bed back among the weeks, and the rows and rows of cans of tomatoes, and piccalilli that she had virtuously preserved. Ariel and Jud caught hands and their faces broke into a blaze of glory. To look at them one could only think of a psalm of praise.

The judge, in his judicial chair, with all his life of wonders and horrors behind him, passed from a momentary astonishment into a twinkle, for he was Irish, and here was the dead come to speak for herself and tell who had killed her. Afterward, as he thought of the entrance, he could liken it to nothing save the sound of the unfolding of soft gray wings, and the look of a little gray dove he had once seen unfurl from the tower of the City Hall, and arrive on the pavement below.

Somehow the routine of the court got all mixed up for a few seconds, and nobody did anything just in accordance with the red tape of justice. But when the excitement began to quiet down, a little man with a brogue, in the back of the room piped up:

"Well, then, yer Honor, who *did* die and git murdered, if it wasn't Miss Dillon? Fer I was there, an' I saw the corpse with my own eyes as shure as I'm aloive, an' it was a dead livin' woman if I iver laid eyes on wan!"

"How about that, Mrs. Granniss?" asked the judge facetiously. "I thought you told us you were sure beyond any possibility of doubt that the dead woman was Miss Dillon."

"You know, yourself, your—*Honor*," snapped Harriet irately, "that I had no means of judging except by the clothes. She certainly had on Emily's skirt—that black serge with the hair line of white you know, Emily," she appealed, haughtily. "I looked for a tiny little tear in the side breadth where Emily caught it on the box the grocer-boy left standing—I was sure she hadn't mended it and it was there. *That's* how I knew it!"

She lifted stubborn eyes to the judge's amused face.

But in Emily's eyes there was a dawning a wistful sadness and light of understanding.

"I gave that skirt to Rebecca Ford," she said, lifting her eyes to the judge's face.

Her lawyer rose excitedly.

"Perhaps that accounts for the fact that we could not find her anywhere when we wanted her for a witness, your Honor," he said.

"This matter must be looked into," said the judge, gravely. "This Rebecca Ford, she was—your washerwoman, I believe, Miss Dillon?"

"She was my *lifelong friend*," said Emily proudly with a shining look misty with tears, and defiant with love which she turned from the judge straight toward Harriet Granniss. "I must look her up at once," said Emily, gently, "my husband and I want to take her home with us. She is not well."

Everybody started and turned toward the tall stranger in surprise. The judge looked him over with a satisfied glance, and then looked down at the little gray woman:

"I'm afraid," he said, gently, "that she has already *gone home!* But we shall see."

Standing upon their chairs, twisting their necks and stretching to see, the people crowded, trying to get a glimpse of Emily Dillon and her husband; chattering like so many magpies about the way the Glenside Tragedy had turned out; nudging one another violently with chameleon-sympathy as Ariel and Jud went seraphically by, arm in arm, going to the little stone bungalow to talk it over and get a breath after the horror; nudging one another with a sneer and a giggle and a final contempt as Harriet Granniss stalked by with the Boggs girl, hands in pockets, gum in jaw, diligently on the job.

They watched until Emily and her tall husband got into an automobile and drove away, and then they followed fast to find out if they were going to Harriet's house, or after Ariel and Jud, or just going loftily back to the city hotel. But the car turned down a side street and sped away so fast they lost it after all. When they were all gone, slowly, thoughtfully, down the marble steps came the judge, hat in hand. He was remembering a little golden-haired girl with blue eyes that he used to know long ago. And down from the court-house tower there floated a little gray dove with white linings to her wings, a canny eye, gray feet, and rose ripples on her neck.

The judge looked down and smiled.

CHAPTER XXVI

LITTLE Dick Smalley's sturdy frame had been worn thin with anxiety during the days that preceded the trial. While the interest of the town centered in the court-house Dick had been alert and inexhaustible. He and Stubby were on hand at the door ready for service at any hour of the day, and the lawyers learned to know his freckled, anxious face. But only Emily Dillon's lawyer dared ask a favor of him, for they had learned by experience where his sympathy lay, and that he would not lift a finger for any other, be it Dillon or Granniss or Boggs. He scorned them all.

He had scarcely slept at all for nights, tossing and finally brought to the extremity of thumping his grimy knees down on the bare floor and trying to pray; though his petition was more in the nature of advice than prayer.

While the actual trial was going on he would not eat, and his lean body was growing almost emaciated. He looked white and drawn and more than one looked at him passing and said: "That boy looks sick." Yet nothing could abate his energy in service.

And when the great ending of the trial had come so suddenly and unexpectedly, it was Dick who had first espied Emily from his post at the court-house door where he was alternating between retreat from fear of hearing the worst, and approach because he couldn't keep away.

The car that brought Emily and her husband to the door of the court-house swept up and Dick swept down simultaneously, and swung the car door open for her with the air of having been waiting for this exact moment for days. And Emily, with all her eagerness to hasten, turned to her husband:

"Oh, Nate, this is Dick. And there is Stubby! Dear Stubby!" Then remembering, anxiously, "Are we in time, Dick?"

"Yep. Just on the dot. Get a hustle on. The other team's makin' a last home run. But you'll can 'em all right! Oh, gee!" and Dick's cap went up in the air with one triumphant fling. He caught it as he ran and was in time up the steps to swing the door noiselessly before them. And so, in breathless wonder, he stood and saw the final act of the tragedy that had turned suddenly into a comedy.

But when the end had come and they looked around for Dick because he had been so a part of Ariel's and Jud's plans for the last three days that they could not even rejoice without him. Dick had disappeared.

Down one street after another went Dick, his nimble feet fairly flying and not far behind, Stubby, spinning away like a streak, his weak foot held in the air as much as might be; straight over hedges and through devious ways, till they came to the back door of Harriet Granniss' abode. Stealthily and swiftly he climbed the neat steps, exulting in their cleanliness, and grasped the top of the garbage can, flinging it down into the velvety grass beneath, Stubby wagging approval below. Out went Dick's hand to the hook, and he had almost made the motion which would have flung the contents of that pail once more over the cleanly scrubbed porch, when a sudden thought arrested him.

He paused, the weight of the heavy pail in his hands. That wasn't the kind of thing those two he loved would do, or would like. Those *three* he might say, for Miss Emily wouldn't approve it either. It *ought* to be done. He would like to do it. But he couldn't do it for their sakes. He had begun to go to Sunday School as soon as Ariel began to teach and he knew a lesson about vengeance and that it wasn't his business, it was God's. That's what all three of his friends would say. That's what God would say. And God had answered his prayer. He hadn't expected it at all—but He *had answered it*. He, just Dick, not even a Christian had had an important prayer answered and this wasn't *fair* to treat God this way—!

Slowly, deliberately, he lifted the dead weight of the can and swung it back on the hook, more slowly he retraced his steps down to the grass, picked up the cover and replaced it on its can. He paused. He couldn't bear to have that woman go without a sign how people thought of her—And yet! Well? There was that coal-of-fire business they had in Sunday School a while back! Why not try that? That was legitimate. But where find a coal? He knit his brows and then was off again across the back fence, across the fields, the railroad track, and down to the flower beds where he ducked behind the station shed and gathered wildly armfuls of late asters, blue and white and purple and pink, from the beautiful station flower beds.

He tore up the last by the roots removing the length of stems as he fled back again. He searched in his pocket for string and tied them to the front door knob, escaping just in time, Stubby and all, as Harriet Granniss, unattended, rounded the corner and came to her lonely door. The Boggs girl had gone off with their lawyer on a joy ride.

Harriet paused, as she came up the steps, looked perplexed a moment; put out her hand to throw the flowers angrily away, then drew them carefully from their binding and looked at them strangely touched. *Where*

had they come from? *Why* had they come? They were
the only sweet and pleasant thing that had come into
her life in many a long day. She buried her grim old
face in their sweet cool fragrance and brought them into
the house, and while she placed them carefully in
water the tears were raining down her cheeks. Who
knows but the ice in her heart too was breaking up, for
the flowers had touched what no punishment or blows
had ever reached. Dick's coal had found its place of
burning.

Jud and Ariel had gone straight to their little house.
Without putting it into words they had gone of one
accord; and standing there together before their own
hearth they looked into each other's eyes with awe.

It was a long time before they spoke, and then Jud,
with his arms close about Ariel said in low earnest tones:

"Ariel, you've won. It's true. He *did* care for us! I
believed it and now I *know* it. This morning I read a
strange new verse: It said, 'He shall give His angels
charge over thee to keep thee in all thy ways,' and I
almost felt like sneering. Then I made up my mind I
wouldn't. I *would* trust even if this were the end! And
now He's proved it true!"

And Ariel lifted her eyes full of joy and said:

"It would have been true anyway, no matter how it
had come out! But oh, I'm so glad it has come out this
way!"

Outside they heard the sound of a car, and Emily and
her husband came driving up, with Dick on flying feet
and Stubby just behind.

"Why can't we be married right here, now, dear?" said
Jud, "Dick'll go and get the minister," he raised his
voice, "Won't you, Dick?"

"Sure thing," sang out Dick Smalley's weary young
voice alertly, "What is't you want?"

Ariel smiled through the mist of joy in her eyes and
said tenderly:

"Jud, I think he's been one of God's angels, don't you?"

And Jud answered fervently as Dick entered breathlessly: "He certainly has."

Heartwarming Books
of
Faith and Inspiration

☐ **THE GOSPEL ACCORDING TO PEANUTS**
Robert L. Short   2070 • $1.25

☐ **NEW MOON RISING** Eugenia Price   2336 • $1.50

☐ **BLESS THIS HOUSE** Anita Bryant   2568 • $1.50

☐ **THE LATE GREAT PLANET EARTH** Hal Lindsey   2666 • $1.75

☐ **THE TRYST** Grace Livingston Hill   2705 • $1.25

☐ **MINE EYES HAVE SEEN THE GLORY** Anita Bryant 2833 • $1.50

☐ **THE WOMAN AT THE WELL** Dale Evans Rogers   2866 • $1.50

☐ **THE GREATEST SALESMAN IN THE WORLD**
Og Mandino   2930 • $1.75

☐ **I'VE GOT TO TALK TO SOMEBODY, GOD**
Marjorie Holmes   2936 • $1.75

☐ **LOVE AND LAUGHTER** Marjorie Holmes   7348 • $1.25

☐ **LIGHTHOUSE** Eugenia Price   7382 • $1.25

☐ **WHO AM I GOD?** Marjorie Holmes   7608 • $1.25

☐ **TWO FROM GALILEE** Marjorie Holmes   7666 • $1.50

☐ **HOW TO TALK TO GOD WHEN YOU AREN'T**
FEELING RELIGIOUS Charles Smith   7712 • $1.25

☐ **THE TASTE OF NEW WINE** Keith Miller   7809 • $1.25

☐ **THEY CALL ME COACH** John Wooden   8146 • $1.50

Buy them at your local bookstore or use this handy coupon for ordering:

Novels of Enduring Romance and Inspiration by

GRACE LIVINGSTON HILL

☐	WHERE TWO WAYS MET	2127	$1.25
☐	SUNRISE	2160	$1.25
☐	BLUE RUIN	2246	$1.25
☐	THE STRANGE PROPOSAL	2252	$1.25
☐	BY WAY OF THE SILVERTHORNS	2258	$1.25
☐	A GIRL TO COME HOME TO	2269	$1.25
☐	THE BELOVED STRANGER	2333	$1.25
☐	APRIL GOLD	2381	$1.25
☐	PARTNERS	2396	$1.25
☐	COMING THROUGH THE RYE	2654	$1.25
☐	THE TRYST	2705	$1.25
☐	THE SEARCH	2711	$1.25
☐	A NEW NAME	6488	$1.25
☐	SPICE BOX	7948	$1.25
☐	HEAD OF THE HOUSE	8547	$1.25
☐	DAWN OF THE MORNING	8799	$1.25

Bantam Book Catalog

It lists over a thousand money-saving best-sellers originally priced from $3.75 to $15.00 —bestsellers that are yours now for as little as 60¢ to $2.95!

The catalog gives you a great opportunity to build your own private library at huge savings!

So don't delay any longer—send us your name and address and 25¢ (to help defray postage and handling costs).